POINT SPREAD

Leaning forw... ...nto the halfback wit... ...ard the familiar sound o... ...eard the grunt of the halfback with all the ... ...ng out of him. The halfback collapsed on his side with Lou driving him into the ground.

Getting to his feet, Lou looked at the sideline marker and glanced at the referee. The halfback had not gained a single inch—no gain.

"Thomas J. Dygard is consistently one of the ablest writers of teenage sports fiction."   —*Booklist*

PUFFIN BOOKS BY THOMAS J. DYGARD

POINT SPREAD

THOMAS J. DYGARD

Puffin Books

PUFFIN BOOKS
Published by the Penguin Group
Viking Penguin, a division of Penguin Books USA Inc.,
375 Hudson Street, New York, New York 10014, U.S.A.
Penguin Books Ltd, 27 Wrights Lane, London W8 5TZ, England
Penguin Books Australia Ltd, Ringwood, Victoria, Australia
Penguin Books Canada Ltd, 10 Alcorn Avenue, Toronto, Ontario, Canada M4V 3B2
Penguin Books (N.Z.) Ltd, 182–190 Wairau Road, Auckland 10, New Zealand

Penguin Books Ltd, Registered Offices: Harmondsworth, Middlesex, England

First published in the United States of America
by William Morrow and Company, Inc., 1980
Published in Puffin Books, 1991
1 3 5 7 9 10 8 6 4 2
Copyright © Thomas J. Dygard, 1980
All rights reserved

Library of Congress Catalog Card Number: 91–53104
ISBN 0-14-034591-4

Printed in the United States of America
Set in Times Roman

For my son, Tom.

1

At the time, Lou Powers did not give the man a second thought. The stranger was small, slender, with a sad-eyed smile, his thin, straight hair slicked down, wearing a beige trenchcoat against the first nip of the advancing Indiana autumn. He fell into step with Lou as he walked across the Meridian University campus.

For Lou Powers, an all-American linebacker with the powerhouse Meridian Browns football team, there was nothing unusual about an encounter with a stranger on the campus. Lou understood, as did most of the standout players, that the fans got a thrill out of exchanging pleasantries for a moment with an all-American football player. Lou was used to the routine. He paid little attention, other than trying to maintain an air of courteous interest as he walked to his next class.

For a young man of his size—six feet, five inches tall, weighing two hundred and fifty-two pounds—Lou walked with a surprising gracefulness. Broad-shouldered, narrow-hipped, thick-legged, he moved with the easy, relaxed flow of the natural athlete.

On this morning in late September there was an extra bounce in Lou's step. Everything in Lou Powers' world seemed perfect. For one thing, there was the cover on this week's issue of *Sports Illustrated* magazine. Right there, in full color, was Lou Powers' picture—a smiling face with high cheekbones and a strong jaw beneath heavy, dark eyebrows, topped by a short crop of curly, black hair. And best of all, the black headline superimposed on the bottom of the color picture: *Best Linebacker in America*.

The story on the inside pages had been flattering. The writer suggested that Lou Powers might—just might—become the first linebacker in history to win the Heisman Trophy. The award distinguishing the nation's best college football player almost always went to a runner or a passer. Defensive players seldom even finished high when the votes of the nation's sportswriters were tallied. Lou was being mentioned as a possibility, which in itself was a glowing honor. The writer suggested also, in stronger terms, that Lou Powers was almost certain to be the first choice in the professional football draft. For Lou, with high hopes of an outstanding professional football career, being chosen first in the pro draft would be the equal of the Heisman Trophy—a great honor. The cover picture and the story had been a thrill.

8

There was a lot of good-natured needling from his teammates. Lou fielded the jokes with what he hoped was an agreeable mixture of indifference and humility. He smiled a lot, and he shrugged a lot.

An assistant coach, obviously concerned with the possibility of Lou's developing a swelled head, growled, "Don't believe everything you read, Powers!"

Lou replied with a smile, "That's what my father told me." An all-American last year, named "Lineman of the Week" three times by the AP, Lou had handled his share of accolades and adulation. He was going to have no trouble with this latest wave of publicity and praise.

But there was more than a full-color magazine cover and a few flattering paragraphs putting a smile on Lou Powers' face this morning. The Meridian Browns, with one victory already under their belts, were headed for a great season. The signs were clear: an undefeated season and the mythical national championship of collegiate football.

Back in the spring, the newspapers and magazines began pegging the Browns as the leading contenders for the national championship. They were doing so even before the sensational Jackie Manteno, one of the nation's most sought-after high-school quarterbacks, chose Meridian for his collegiate career.

Then, last week, in the annual preseason rankings, the Browns stood at the top—the No. 1 choice of the sportswriters and sportscasters voting in the AP poll and the coaches voting in the UPI poll. Jackie Manteno still had not stepped onto the field to play a game. When the

9

cocky, fast-talking freshman passed for three touchdowns in leading the Browns to their 42–0 victory over Norring Tech in the season's opener, all doubt vanished. A powerful contender before Jackie Manteno enrolled, and now with the added firepower of the spectacular newcomer at quarterback, the Browns appeared to be a shoo-in for the national championship.

Lou regretted Brad Chapman's being knocked out of the signal-caller job in his senior year. But Lou could not argue with the coaches' decision. Brad Chapman was a great quarterback, for sure. But Jackie Manteno was a shade greater.

The Browns' defense, led by Lou Powers from his middle linebacker position, performed flawlessly in shutting out Norring Tech. The goose-egg victory marked the first step toward fulfilling a secret dream of Lou's: a season of shutouts, a Meridian defense giving up no points at all. Such a record had never been accomplished in the history of magnificent defenses at Meridian.

"You look happy this morning," the man said, walking alongside Lou on the brick courtyard in front of the field house.

The remark snapped Lou out of his thoughts. "What?"

"I said that you look happy this morning." The man was smiling up at Lou.

"Yes, it's a beautiful morning."

"You really whacked Norring Tech. A lot worse than anyone expected. Everybody knew you were loaded this year. But that much?"

Lou looked at the man. He was sure that he did not know him. Yet there was something familiar about the face. The slightly bulging eyes in the flat, round face, the hair combed straight across, the sad expression behind the fixed smile. It was not a pleasant face, to be sure, but a distinctive one, and somehow familiar. Lou tried to remember where he had seen it. Suddenly it dawned on him. The face was out of a television movie Lou had seen only a few nights ago. It was the face of the actor, Peter Lorre. The man looked like Peter Lorre. Lou wondered if anyone ever had told him that.

The man kept talking. "Danton is going to be tougher, maybe even tougher than people think," he said.

The game with the Danton Buccaneers, second team on the Browns' schedule, was only three days away. Yes, the Buccaneers were going to be tough. Lou recalled his games against the Buccaneers the last three years. Always a national power, the Buccaneers played a wild and wide-open style of game featuring a lot of passing, zany reverses, and unorthodox spread formations. They had the talent to make the tricks work. The Buccaneers were a scoring threat from any position on the field at any time. Their unpredictability made them a challenge of the toughest sort for a linebacker. Doubtless, Lou Powers and his Meridian defense were in for a difficult afternoon.

"Danton is always tough," Lou said. "But we'll be ready."

The man seemed interested in Lou's remark. "So

everybody's healthy then? No injuries left over from the Norring Tech game?"

Lou glanced down at the man as they walked along together. Something about his manner gave Lou an uneasy feeling. There was something vaguely troubling about him. Lou wondered who he was. He was not a sportswriter. That much was certain. The sportswriters always introduced themselves. Nor did the man fit the picture of the old grad. True, old grads came in all shapes and sizes. They were fat and skinny, rich and poor, tall and short, smiling and frowning. Perhaps some even looked like Peter Lorre. But Lou was sure the man was not a Meridian alumnus. The usual fans were more interested in discussing last week's triumph—reliving the joy of the victory—than in talking about next week's prospects. This man had led the conversation toward the upcoming Danton game without delay. And now he wanted to know about any injuries among the Browns.

"No, we'll be ready," Lou said.

"Still, Danton is going to be tough, maybe tougher than anybody figures."

"Yes," Lou said. He wished the man would leave.

"The card says you'll beat them by twenty-two points —better than three touchdowns. I figure closer than that. I know that you guys are loaded this year. But I still figure a closer score. I say that it will be Meridian by a couple of touchdowns, but no more. Fourteen points, say. What do you think?"

Lou gave the man a sideways look. So that was it! The man was a bettor, looking for an edge. People everywhere bet on football games. Lou knew it. People play the football cards. They buy into pools in their offices and guess the point spread. They wager with friends in taverns, country clubs, across the back fence—everywhere. Lou knew about it. The betting was harmless, friendly wagering. And this man wanted to protect his ten-spot.

"I've got to run for a class," Lou said.

He broke into a gentle jog toward the Business Administration building, leaving the man behind.

Turning the corner of the building and approaching the door, Lou glanced back. The man was standing there, the fixed smile still in place.

2

At Meridian University, there always was an extra crackle in the air for the season's first game in the old limestone and brick stadium, scene of more than a hundred of the greatest college football games ever played. Having opened their season on the West Coast against Norring Tech, the Browns' game with the Danton Buccaneers was the home opener. The fans were getting their first look at this year's edition of football greatness in a brown uniform.

Already the stadium was filling. The weather was perfect for football: slightly overcast, neither cloudy nor sunny; almost windless, with only the faintest hint of a breeze; cool, brisk. The snap of autumn was in the air.

On the field, the Browns were jogging under the goal-

14

posts, cutting to the sideline and circling back at mid-field to the end zone, settling into rows from sideline to sideline for light calisthenics.

Lou glanced up at the rows of seats. By the moment of the kickoff, not a vacant seat would remain. The attendance figure, always announced as the same, would be 62,010, full capacity for the old stadium. Nobody's memory reached back far enough to recall an empty seat at a Browns' home game.

On the cinder track beyond the sideline, the television crews were placing themselves and testing equipment. Meridian vs. Danton was television's game of the week.

All week the television network had billed the game as a classic struggle between differing football styles exemplified by two of the nation's gridiron titans. On the one side, there was the balanced and dazzling offense of the Danton Buccaneers. On the other, there was the legendary Meridian Browns' defense, led this year by Lou Powers, the nation's best linebacker, a candidate for the Heisman Trophy. The unstoppable force was facing the immovable object.

At the other end of the field, Lou saw the Danton Buccaneers moving into position for their warm-up calisthenics. The Buccaneers were wearing their white uniforms with bright-green numerals and trim. They had flown into Indianapolis from their Texas campus last night and taken chartered buses this morning for the short ride into Meridian. They had the muscle kinks of travel to iron out. Lou knew the feeling.

15

Coach Buck Foster, always the last man out of the Browns' dressing room, passed into Lou's line of sight on the field. Foster was slender—the same weight he'd carried as a Meridian defensive end twenty years before —with a beak nose and large, wire-rimmed spectacles. He wore brown slacks, an open-neck sport shirt, and a brown sweater, in the tradition of Meridian Browns' coaches. At the moment he was heading for the middle of the field, where his assistant coaches already were gathered to watch the warm-up drills.

Foster's usual deep frown was in place as he strode across the natural turf of the playing field. Foster was famous for the frown. Even in his playing days, he always was frowning. His picture on the wall with the other Meridian all-American players at the Brown House restaurant on the edge of the campus provided ample evidence. In the pictures mounted on the wall behind the bar, most of the players were smiling. But not Foster. He was scowling into the camera. He looked more like a premed student worried about his grades than a skillful tackler just named to the all-American team.

In Foster's first year as head coach, five years ago, when he guided the Browns to the national championship, a sportswriter had quipped in print: "There were rumors circulating on the Meridian campus today that Buck Foster smiled. The rumors could not be confirmed."

With each passing year Lou understood better the

pressures that kept Buck Foster frowning as head coach of the Browns.

In a way, winning the national championship in his first season at the helm was a stroke of bad luck for Buck Foster. The Browns' fans cheered the great triumph—a return to the old days of glory—and then expected another championship the next year, and one each year thereafter. But there had been no more national championships for Buck Foster and the Meridian Browns since that first year. Last year, for example, the Browns had lost two games. True, the losses were by one point in one game and two points in the other. But still they were losses. And at Meridian, with the ghosts of champions lurking everywhere, an 8–2 won-lost record was accepted as a losing season. Nobody won the national championship with two losses. At Meridian, loss of the national championship was a losing season.

This year the Browns had outstanding player material, perhaps their best in a decade. They had depth, talent, and strength. Everybody knew it. Lou knew it. All the players knew it. Buck Foster knew it. The whole world knew it. And the simple, undisputed fact added to the pressures on Buck Foster. With great material, the coach was expected to deliver a winner. And at Meridian, a winner meant the national championship.

This year, too, was the first Browns' team peopled entirely by Buck Foster's players. The seniors, such as Lou, were the high-school graduates the year Foster first took over the Meridian Browns. This year, for the first time, *every* player on the squad was a player Foster had selected and accepted. Every player had been coached in the Foster system through all of his collegiate playing days, which added to the pressures on Buck Foster too.

Foster understood. He was blunt when answering the questions of the sportswriters and sportscasters: "The national championship is our goal every year, and this season is no different." Period.

The players, in their rows across the end of the field, finished their calisthenics. Otis Hildegard, the defensive coach, broke away from the knot of coaches standing at midfield and headed for the sideline. Lou and the other members of the defense moved over with him. Bernie Carlisle, the backfield coach, walked toward the other sideline, joining his offense unit for dummy play drills.

All around the bowl of the stadium, the blank spaces were filling in with a solid mass of brown. No Meridian fan worth the name wore any other color to a Meridian game. The small crowd of Danton fans, wearing green and white, fluttering their pennants, stood out in sharp contrast in their section of the stadium.

At the far end of the field, in the corner behind the Danton Buccaneers, a dozen members of the Meridian band belted out a fight song.

Foster paced back and forth between the offense and the defense units. He appeared oblivious to the noise of the crowd and the band, unaware of the television camera following him every step of the way. Foster glared at the defensive players, blocking and bumping

18

into each other. He frowned at the offense, moving down the field with a series of plays run at half speed.

Later, in the dressing room, in the final moment before taking the field for the kickoff, Foster stepped into the center of the floor. He waited a moment for silence.

"Just a word now," he said. "Remember this: You *are* the Meridian Browns."

Every one of the Meridian Browns' coaches, going back as far as anyone knew, had made the same simple statement before each game. It was the last sentence heard by generations of Meridian Browns football players heading into the opening kickoff. The simple statement never failed to conjure up in Lou's mind the vision of the Meridian Browns the first time he saw them play a football game.

Lou Powers was a high-school senior, the first player in the history of Oklahoma high-school football ever to be named to both the offensive and defensive units of the all-state team. He was a bone-jarring fullback on offense, a quick and strong linebacker on defense.

For the Oklahoma Sooners, who so dearly wanted Lou's strength and talent, there was great irony in the fact that the Sooners themselves were the ones who first exposed Lou to the Meridian Browns.

The two national powers, the Browns and the Sooners, were playing at Norman, and Lou's father had taken him to the game. The Browns won the game, and more. They won the heart of the sturdy young athlete who played both fullback and linebacker for his high-school team.

Although few knew it, and even fewer understood, Lou's love was defense. He preferred the play at line-backer—the mental challenge of anticipating the opponents' next play, the physical test of fighting through blockers and tackling a runner. This skill, to Lou, was the glory of football. In his mind the thrill of carrying the ball, even of scoring a touchdown, paled in comparison.

Sitting in the grandstand alongside his father on that day four years ago, Lou had watched the Meridian defense. They were marvelous. They were tough, disciplined, expert—and proud. They made a drama of every play. They drew strength from the storied Meridian defenses of the past years. At one point, they stopped the Sooners in their tracks on fourth down with two inches to go for a first down. Lou's eyes were glistening as he watched the Meridian defensive unit walk off the field, having done their job. They were the best, and they knew it. Their pride showed in the way they walked. Their predecessors had been the best. And now, once again, the magnificent tradition had been upheld. Lou had felt a tingle of pride for them. If only someday he could play linebacker for the Meridian Browns and become a part of that great tradition. . . .

The old tingling sensation returned now as Foster spoke the words. Foster paused a second after speaking, then nodded at Lou. As defensive captain, Lou had the role of leading the Browns onto the field for the start of the game.

Lou leaped off the bench and jogged through the

door. The other players crowded through the door behind him. Coming out of the ramp and onto the field, Lou lifted his right fist above his head and broke into a full-tilt run toward the bench, leading the horde of Meridian players.

The brown-clad people in the stadium rose as one with a roaring cheer.

3

A dream ended for Lou Powers late in the first quarter. The Danton Buccaneers scored a touchdown.

For the first twelve minutes of the game, the two teams battered each other at midfield. Neither offense was able to penetrate beyond the thirty-five-yard line. Neither team's defense was able to come up with the big play that shoved the opponent back into its own territory. The two teams probed and punched, passed and ran—and got nowhere. The physical pounding was tremendous. The rewards were slight.

Then Danton, on the Browns' thirty-eight-yard line, took a time-out. The quarterback jogged to the sideline.

The Danton coach, wearing headphones connecting him to a spotter in the press box, had called for the time-out. Why? Clearly, the spotter in the press box had seen something—what?—in the Meridian defense worth talking about. The coach was passing the information on to his quarterback.

The quarterback conferred only a moment with his coach and returned to the huddle on the field. The play was third down with three yards to go for a first down. For most teams, the next play was an easy choice: the best ballcarrier running behind the best blocker to get the first down. But Danton frequently ignored the logical tactic in favor of a surprise. The Buccaneers were gamblers in their play selection. They had the muscle and skill to make their gambles pay off. Their daring style of play was what had kept them high in the national rankings over the years. There was no telling what was coming up from the Buccaneers now.

The time-out increased Lou's anxiety. The Buccaneers always were a tough riddle on offense. Now, in addition, something special seemed to be coming up.

In the stands the Meridian fans were on their feet. They, too, sensed that Danton was reaching into the hat, looking for a rabbit. One of the Buccaneer's patented magic tricks was about to be performed. The rhythmic roar of "Deee-fense! Deee-fense!" rolled down onto the playing field from all sides of the stadium. The situation was a classic one for the Browns' defense, and tradition dictated that the Browns jam the corridors, block the pass, halt the attackers in their tracks, force the opponent to punt the ball away.

Lou glanced at his partners in the defense. They were ready.

The Buccaneers came out of the huddle and lined up. Their linemen were spread slightly wider than usual. In the backfield, two flankers were out wide, one to each side. The fullback was leaning forward in his position behind the quarterback.

The possibilities clicked through Lou's mind. The linemen, spread wide, seemed to be inviting Lou to blitz through into the backfield from his linebacker position. That might mean a pass—into the zone he left vacant in order to blitz. A screen pass, short and quick, over the heads of the defensive linemen charging through, was a deadly weapon. Lou eyed the two flankers. They were positioned for a pass. They might float out and take a pass at the sideline, or they might cut across the center for a pass in Lou's zone. And then, too, there was the fullback, poised to spring from his position. The widespread linemen, inviting a charge, might well be setting up a draw play, designed to slip the charging fullback past the onrushing Browns' linemen.

As the long list of possibilities danced through Lou's mind, he glanced around again at his teammates in the defense. The Browns' defensive halfbacks were moving out to cover the flankers. Lou's partners at linebacker, Henry Alderman to his left and Marion Petoskey to his right, were moving out a pace also, widening the area assigned to Lou in the center. With Lou's speed and savvy, they were safe in giving him more territory to cover. They were correct in widening the defense against the threat of the flankers. In front of Lou, the Browns' front four—the two guards and the two tackles—were bracing for their charge.

Lou decided quickly that the front four were able to breach the wide seams of the Buccaneers' widely spaced offensive line. The front four were the ones to charge into the Buccaneers' backfield. Lou was not going to blitz. He was going to guard his area. He was a free-lancer, counting on his instincts to take him in the direction of the play, once it began to unfold. He was a rover on defense.

The Danton quarterback was barking his signals.

Lou, four yards behind the line of scrimmage, staring at the quarterback, rocked slightly on the balls of his feet. He was leaning forward, hands out, ready. The quarterback was watching him. Lou gave no sign of his plan—blitz, or backpedal for a pass, or hold his ground to chase a ballcarrier. A good linebacker is every bit the actor that a good quarterback is.

The Buccaneers' quarterback took the snap, turned, and faked a hand-off to the fullback charging over guard. The move froze Lou in his position momentarily, as it was designed to do. But the momentary hesitation did not matter. Lou was not committing himself until he knew where the play was going.

Still turning, the quarterback shoveled the ball backward to the flanker now racing across the field in a deep arc through the backfield from Lou's left.

The play surprised Lou. The flanker had a long run to get himself into position to receive the lateral at full speed. The play, eating up seconds, was risky. Every second that passed increased the chances of one of the Browns' front four crashing through for the tackle. Too, the flanker was giving up yardage in his run across the field in order to keep himself beyond the grasp of any tackler breaking through into the backfield. The flanker was fully ten yards behind the line of scrimmage when he gathered in the lateral.

The daring of the deep-starting play impressed Lou. The flanker now needed to gain thirteen yards in his sweep around the opposite end to make the first down— ten yards to get himself back to the line of scrimmage and three to win the first down.

Max Schellenbarger, from his left tackle position, slammed the quarterback to the ground just as the lateral went spiraling back into the flanker's hands.

Henry Alderman was coming in fast behind the flanker and then suddenly disappeared, cut down by a blocker.

Lou moved to his right, following the flow of the play. He moved cautiously, half expecting the flanker to cut sharply off tackle on a straight line upfield for the yardage needed for the first down. But the flanker remained on course, speeding toward the opposite side-line, angling upfield as he went. The flanker was going to reach the line of scrimmage in a moment. Lou turned on the speed and headed for the ballcarrier. The other brown jerseys in the defense were in the crowd now. Danton blockers materialized suddenly. Lou, his legs driving, his hands working furiously to shove the bodies aside, battled his way toward the ballcarrier. He stumbled, stepped over a player, and kept going.

Then suddenly, out of the corner of his eye, Lou saw the ball in the air. He knew instantly what was happening. The speeding flanker was dropping off a lateral to the other flanker, heading back the other way. Just as suddenly the Buccaneers' blockers eased up. They let the Browns' tacklers charge through—the wrong way, going away from the runner now carrying the ball.

Lou slammed on the brakes and turned. He had been fooled. The Buccaneers had lured him into the wrong commitment. The execution of the play was perfect. They stretched out Lou's caution until it broke. Then, at precisely the proper instant, they turned the play around. The flanker was on his way, sailing through the remnants of the scattered Browns' defense.

Henry Alderman, regaining his feet from the block that knocked him out of the early moments of the play, made a lunging reach for the flanker speeding past him. But the flanker was too quick. He was a step away from Henry's grasp.

In a horrible flash, Lou saw his dream of holding every team scoreless through the entire season evaporating before his eyes. But maybe not.

Lou stiff-armed the shoulder pads of a blocker plunging toward him and began the race downfield in pursuit of the ballcarrier.

The ballcarrier, untouched so far, was making his

turn and scampering along the sideline. He slowed his pace slightly, and expertly, to allow a blocker to get between himself and the Browns' defensive halfback, who was trying to recover from being sucked out of position. The blocker cut down the off-balance halfback easily. The flanker danced around the pile of bodies and shifted into high gear again, resuming his race for the goal. There was nothing between him and the goal.

Lou, free now of the tangle of blockers, turned on the speed. He ran with every ounce of his strength. The flanker's momentary pause to get around the defensive halfback gave Lou a bonus. He gained a step in his pursuit.

Lou angled toward the sideline, aiming for a collision with the runner at the five-yard line.

In the stands, the crowd remained on their feet. The fans had been shocked by the Buccaneers' spectacular reverse. Now they were entranced by the duel of speed unfolding before them on the field.

The race was on. The ballcarrier was crossing the twenty-yard line. Lou, with his speed of 4.9 seconds in the forty-yard dash, was angling in on him, closing the gap.

Lou sensed that the Buccaneer was winning the contest. He was going to cross the goal line before Lou could intercept him. Lou veered his course a couple of degrees and concentrated on catching him.

He did. But the runner fell over the goal line in Lou's arms, and the referee threw his arms skyward—touchdown!

The scoreboard flickered and settled into place: Browns 0, Visitors 6.

A moment later it was: Browns 0, Visitors 7.

The walk to the bench was a long one for Lou. He picked up a parka and slung it loosely over his shoulders. Standing with his arms folded, he stared across the field.

4

By the half time the Browns had tied the score at 7–7.
They piled on two more touchdowns in the third quarter
and held on for a 21–7 triumph over the Danton Buccaneers.

Nowhere in the scoring summary of the game was the
name of Lou Powers listed. He gained no yards rushing
from scrimmage. He did not carry the ball for a touchdown or even for a first down. He threw no passes, and
he caught none.

Not one of the sportswriters typing in the press box
mentioned Lou Powers' name in the first paragraph of
his story. Not a single headline writer at any newspaper
in the country was going to spell out Lou Powers' name
for the black banner headlines proclaiming another
great Meridian Browns football victory.

The offense, not the defense, scored the points that won the game.

Jackie Manteno, the Browns' sensational freshman quarterback, passed down the field for the first Meridian touchdown, tying the score at 7–7 just before the half.

Jackie's pinpoint passing set up the second Browns' score, with Bull Hoffman, the Browns' thundering fullback, crashing through for the last yard across the goal.

Bull Hoffman's strong running up the middle and Donny Campbell's skittish scampering from his flanker position set up the third touchdown for insurance in the waning minutes of the third quarter.

Furthermore, the Browns finished strong, with a drive for a sure touchdown in the fourth quarter spiked only by the miscue of a single misthrown pass—an interception by the Buccaneers.

The offense provided the loudly proclaimed ingredients of victory for the Browns in their battle with the Danton Buccaneers. But in the jubilant Browns' dressing room, Coach Buck Foster presented the game ball to Lou Powers.

Tradition at Meridian dictated that the game ball be presented after each victory to a player deemed the most valuable. Symbolically the gesture said: "Without you, we could not have won this game."

All schools award the game ball to a player on occasion. If the game is big enough or exciting enough, if the victory dramatic enough, or if the player obviously won the game single-handedly, he receives the game ball. It has to be a clear-cut choice.

But at Meridian all games were big ones. All games were exciting. All of them were dramatic. The Browns took pride in having such depth of team spirit and tradition that one of their number could receive the game ball after each victory, every time, without causing ill feeling.

This was the sixth time that Lou Powers had received the game ball during his career at Meridian. Many times the decision of the coaching staff was a close one. But not this time.

True, Jackie Manteno's passing and masterful ball handling kept the Browns' offense moving in the come-from-behind effort. And true, Spider Willard, from his end position, performed a circus catch when collecting a Manteno pass in the end zone, pulling the Browns up even on the scoreboard late in the second quarter. The touchdown turned the tide and set the tone for the Meridian scores in the third quarter. True, too, Bull Hoffman gained ninety-eight yards rushing with his powerful thrusts through the line, and he scored the Browns' go-ahead touchdown. Donny Campbell, quick and shifty, picked up critical yardage, keeping drives alive through the second half. His twenty-two-yard scamper got the key first down in the Brown's final scoring drive.

But the defense, led by Lou Powers, a hulking figure of surprising speed at the middle linebacker position, were the ones who made it all possible.

One statistic revealed what happened: the Buccaneers' total net rushing yardage at game's end was seventy-two. The Buccaneers gained more than that, to be sure. But they found themselves being thrown back for losses time and again. An eight-yard gain went for naught when they were knocked back for a six-yard loss on the next play. In the end, their total gain stood at seventy-two yards, lowest in memory for the explosive Danton attack. The statistic took on even greater significance considering that the Buccaneers got thirty-eight of those seventy-two yards on one play, the touchdown play in the first quarter. And all this defensive effort was due to the thundering middle linebacker of the Browns.

Lou Powers jammed the holes in the line. He knocked down passes. He chased runners to the ground in their own backfield. He roamed from sideline to sideline, annihilating blockers and destroying ballcarriers. Lou finished the game with sixteen unassisted tackles, six assists on other tackles, one fumble recovery, and one pass interception.

In addition, and probably more important than any accomplishment listed in the statistics, Lou's performance calling the defensive signals for the Browns was uncannily accurate. Almost like magic, he anticipated the Buccaneers' plays, guided his teammates to the right position for the right moves to nail the attackers in their tracks.

Because of Lou and his defense unit, the Browns did not need long drives to punch across their touchdowns. Their scoring drives were short. The Browns' defense relentlessly held the Buccaneers bottled up in their own end of the field, pushed them backward at every turn, forcing them to give up the ball in good field position for the Browns' attackers.

Any offensive player knows full well the difference between midfield and his own five-yard line when taking possession of the ball. It is the difference between high hopes and extreme danger. Lou's defense turned over the ball to the Browns' offense in a position of high hopes every time. The result, as was usually the case with the Browns, was victory in the final score.

"Speech, speech," Donny Campbell shouted, when Lou accepted the game ball from the coach.

Lou grinned. "I hope," he said slowly, holding the ball in both hands, "that this is not the same ball the Buccaneers were using when they scored on that reverse."

Everybody howled with laughter.

Even Buck Foster's face crinkled a bit with a slight smile.

Lou stepped out of the dressing room into the corridor jammed with fans and sportswriters.

Win or lose, Buck Foster allowed neither fans nor sportswriters inside the Browns' dressing room after a game. The coach felt that the flush of victroy or the tears of defeat belonged to the team members—in privacy.

A photographer's strobe light flashed in the heavy shadows of the crowded corridor outside the dressing room

Somebody noticed that Lou was carrying the game

34

ball. "Hey, hold up the ball," a photographer shouted.

Lou lifted the ball in one hand and smiled in the direction of the shouted command. The fans cheered. The light flashed again.

Lou eased his way through the crowd, scanning the edges for the freckled face, the laughing blue eyes, and the blond hair of the girl named Paige Hemphill. He nodded and smiled in acknowledgment of the congratulations of the elated Browns fans as he gently shoved his way through the crush. He saw the sad face of Brad Chapman's father. Mr. Chapman never missed a Browns' game, although his son was relegated to the bench by the sensational Jackie Manteno. Lou nodded to Mr. Chapman.

Lou knew that Paige was waiting somewhere at the edge of the crowd. Paige Hemphill had been waiting for him after games since their sophomore year. She was going to become Mrs. Lou Powers in June, following the day they both stepped forward to take their degrees at commencement. Slowly and good-naturedly, Lou worked his way out.

Paige would lift a hand in a wave when she spotted Lou towering over most of the people around him.

Suddenly the little man with the sad-eyed smile, wearing the same beige trenchcoat, was in front of Lou. The man's face startled Lou.

"Great game," he said. His fixed smile remained in place. "Congratulations."

"Thank you," Lou said.

Lou again felt an uneasy sensation. He was conscious

of something unpleasant about the man. The feeling of their first meeting returned now, stronger than ever. Lou turned and continued to look for Paige.

The man was at Lou's side now. He thrust an envelope into Lou's hand and turned and vanished in the crowd.

Lou took the envelope. He started to call out. But the man was gone.

Without looking at the envelope in his hand, Lou stuffed it into his topcoat pocket. He thought he knew what was inside, and the thought did not please him.

Paige was waving. He could see her face now and waved back.

"Why aren't you smiling?" Paige asked. "Winners are supposed to smile, aren't they?"

5

Lou was not surprised when he found money in the envelope.

He was standing in the center of his room at the Sigma Chi house. He had dropped Paige off at her dormitory to change for their date. Lou was alone, looking at the envelope in his hand. He tossed the envelope onto his desk. It landed with a thump. The picture of the man's sad-eyed, smiling face remained in his mind. He picked up the envelope, hefted it a moment in his right hand, and tore off the end.

Lou slid the stack of bills out of the envelope and into his hand. He tossed the empty envelope back onto the desk and counted the currency.

He was surprised at the amount—five hundred dollars. He recounted the money. There were twenty-five twenty-dollar bills—five hundred dollars.

Lou dropped the stack of crisp bills on the desk. The bills slid into a fan shape. He looked at the money for a moment; then he turned to the window and stared out at the heavy shadows of the early evening.

Standing there, Lou said the word aloud. "Gambler."

The little man with the sad-eyed smile and the beige trenchcoat was not a fan enjoying a brief conversation with an all-American football player walking across the Meridian University campus. He was not a casual bettor, asking where to place his ten-spot in the neighborhood pool. He was not looking for a tip to help him preserve his ten-spot with the boys at the tavern. He was not harmless at all.

Lou knew that the Browns were the subject of large bets all across the country every week of the football season. He read the predictions appearing in the sports pages of the newspapers and saw them listed in the television sportscasts. He knew about the point spread. Some of the predictors were fond of calling their shots by a half point. The Browns will win this Saturday by six *and a half* points. Six *and a half* points? Nobody scores a half point in a football game. The half point is a vehicle for betting. It eliminates the chance of a tie in the wager. Nothing more.

Lou repeated the word. "Gambler."

The thoughts began swirling through his mind. Okay, so the man was a gambler, and he had made a payoff. That was the answer.

But the answer was not the answer at all. Instead of answering the question, it raised a host of new questions. A payoff for what? Lou had done nothing for a gambler.

But, yes, Lou might in the future do something for a gambler.

Was that it? An advance payment on future favors? A clear signal of more money to come? If there was $500 for nothing, how much more would there be for services performed? A lot probably.

Lou knew how the system worked. He knew about the college basketball betting scandals several years before. He knew the arguments the gamblers had used with telling effect on some of the nation's top players. "You don't have to throw the game," the gamblers told the players. "Just keep the score close—close enough." The players were able to rationalize their way out of whatever pangs of guilt they felt. They continued to lead their teams to victory, as they wanted to do, and they collected from the gamblers for holding down the score. The gamblers collected too, because the scores turned out to be closer than anyone—anyone outside the fix, that is—figured they would be.

Lou glanced over his shoulder at the money spread out in a fan shape on his desk.

Were there any other envelopes stuffed with money handed out to Brown players after the Danton game? Jackie Manteno? Donny Campbell? Bull Hoffman? His own partners at linebacker, Marion Petoskey and Henry Alderman? Anyone?

What were they doing right now? Were they counting

the money, alone in a room? Were they wondering, rationalizing? Had they already decided?

Lou's mind went back to last season. Two losses: one by two points, one by one point. Were those losses the result of a point shaver losing his own gamble, holding back too much and losing the game? It was impossible. No, it was possible.

It was all impossible—the man in the trenchcoat, the money, all of it. No, it was possible.

But why Lou Powers?

The question frightened Lou. Had he said something, anything, ever, that had been overheard, leading somebody to think that Lou Powers wanted or needed money badly enough to buy a gambler's deal? Lou could think of nothing. Oh, sure, Lou Powers wanted money as much as any college senior. He was going to be moving out into the world where money was needed. He and Paige were going to be married. They would be wanting the things that money buys: a car, furniture, clothing, maybe a house. But Lou was sure that he never had said anything to anyone indicating that his honor was for sale.

Anyway, why a linebacker? Gamblers want to shave points, keep the score within the bounds of the point spread. But Lou Powers, a linebacker, did not carry the ball. He did not throw passes. He was not a key pass receiver. His job was not to put points on the scoreboard. So how could he shave points?

The gamblers needed a fumble at a critical juncture, a misthrown pass that gets intercepted, a bad hand-off that loses yardage and kills a drive. Those were the things the gambers needed to shave points and win their bets, but they were not the things a linebacker does.

Suddenly the realization hit Lou. But of course a linebacker. The horrible memory of his momentary error allowing the Danton Buccaneers to score a touchdown flashed through his mind. Yes, a linebacker does control the score. A misstep, a miscalculation can spell touchdown for an opponent. An extra touchdown for the underdog, provided by a linebacker's error, has the same effect on the point spread as the favorite's failing to score. Yes, the linebacker. An inch given on a tackle—one inch—can provide a first down, keeping an opponet's drive for the goal alive. The cliché is true: football is a game of inches. The linebacker controls those inches as much as any player on the field.

Okay, so that was why a linebacker. But why this linebacker? Why Lou Powers?

Lou did not like the answer he found: the gambler wanted Lou Powers because Lou Powers could do the job. Lou called the defensive signals for the Meridian Browns. He led the team in tackles. He led the team in pass interceptions. He was the key to the Meridian Browns' defense. The entire defense functioned at his direction, revolved around his performance, succeeded as he succeeded, failed as he failed. He held it all in his hands.

Lou Powers was a great linebacker. By being a bit less than great at certain selected moments—only one or two critical junctures in the game—Lou could deliver

41

what the gambler wanted. Furthermore, Lou knew he could deliver what the gambler wanted without fear of detection.

As a linebacker he was, in fact, in a better position to deliver—and get away with it—than any other player on the team.

An offensive player's errors are committed in the glare of the spotlight. When a quarterback throws an interception, *his* pass is what went wrong. *His* poor hand-off ruins a running play and kills a drive. When any player handling the ball loses it, *his* fumble is the mistake. The errors are obvious, easily attributable, and statistically noted. But a linebacker's errors are a matter of degree. The occasional lapses, if noticed at all, are almost impossible to assess.

Who could say whether Lou Powers allowed Danton to score on a zany reverse or not? Besides, who was going to remember if, in the end, the score turned out right? He could have done so easily. The thought made Lou shiver.

"What in the world is wrong with you tonight?"

Paige was looking up at Lou while they danced to an old-time slow number in the basement of the Sigma Chi house. The postgame party, one of a dozen in fraternity houses dotted around the campus, was nearing an end.

Lou was conscious that Paige had been studying him closely ever since they had met outside the dressing room in the stadium. But still he couldn't wrench his mind away from the envelope.

All evening, first during their dinner at the Brown House and now at the party, the questions swirled through Lou's mind: Why me? Are any other players involved? What am I going to do about it? Lou had to force the smiles acknowledging the shouts of congratulation for the victory. He caught himself repeatedly having to jerk himself back to the present and ask Paige what she had said.

"Well?" Paige persisted. "Something *is* wrong."

Lou gave her a faint smile. "Who, me?"

"You've been a million miles away tonight."

"Nothing is wrong," Lou said. "Just tired, I guess. You know, not in the mood for a party."

"Meaning, I assume, that you're not going to tell me about it."

Lou stopped dancing and took a half step backward from Paige. "Look, forget it, will you?"

Paige blinked up at him.

Lou was instantly sorry he had snapped at her. But he said nothing.

"Let's go," Paige said suddenly. "The party's almost over anyway."

6

As usual during football season, Lou Powers appeared at the field house at six o'clock on Sunday morning.

Coach Foster did not require the players to attend the first viewing of the film of the previous day's game. He did not even encourage the players' attendance. But he allowed it, and usually a few of the Browns showed up to join the coaches in the projection room in the basement of the field house.

Lou, Jackie Manteno, and Brad Chapman were the only regulars. For Lou, the screening was an educational opportunity. He learned by watching himself play. He learned by watching the other players, too. His knowledge of his teammates in the defensive unit was valuable to Lou. Keeping in mind what he knew about them, he made split-second decisions on the field. The decisions often meant win or lose for the Browns at the end of the game. Jackie, still getting used to his new teammates, came for the same reasons. For Brad Chapman, the ritual appearance on Sunday mornings was partly habit built over the last three years. But he also needed to keep himself ready to step in.

Other players varied in their attendance, showing up for any one of a number of personal reasons. Sometimes a player appeared for the screening because he felt his performance the day before had been below par. He wanted to study the replay of his moves on the field. He wanted to hear the coaches' reactions. On occasion, a player with an outstanding game performance behind him attended the screening for the pure pleasure of reliving his moments of triumph.

But Lou had more on his mind than the film of the Danton Buccaneers game as he pulled open the front door of the field house and stepped into the lobby. The envelope, letter-size, of heavy brown manila, with one end torn open, was in his jacket pocket.

Lou rubbed an eye with the back of his hand. He had not slept well. For most of the night he had lain on his back, staring through the darkness toward the ceiling of his room.

The haunting question was not whether to buy the gambler's deal. Sure, he could pull it off. No question about it. Lou could yield, ever so slightly, at a critical juncture. He could narrow the point spread in a game the Browns were winning. He could satisfy the gambler, while the Browns marched on to victory. He did not doubt it. The moment of realization, standing there in his room with the money spread out on the desk, had been frightening for Lou. Holding the score down would be so easy—and so profitable, undoubtedly. But Lou knew that he would not do it. He knew that he would never compromise his place in the hallowed tradition of the Meridian Browns football team. He had lived with the dream too long to sell it out, no matter how much the money.

The question of why a linebacker was answered now. And the question of why *this* linebacker was answered too. But the question of what to do, how to end it all, how to get out was not answered.

At first, the solution seemed simple. Lou would go to Buck Foster, hand over the money, tell the story of what had happened, and then forget the whole episode. Lou would walk away, clean and unworried. Very simple.

But in the darkness of his room, staring at the ceiling, Lou knew that the aftermath would not be so simple. There would be questions. The authorities would be called in. The university administration would get involved. Probably the NCAA would investigate.

There would be suspicions. After all, Lou Powers had accepted the gambler's money, hadn't he?

There would be publicity. Lou Powers was a national figure. Witness the cover picture on *Sports Illustrated* magazine. Lou was known by football fans everywhere. He was news, and there was no escaping the fact.

The publicity would feed the suspicions. In the end, he

46

would become Lou Powers, the linebacker who took an envelope full of twenty-dollar bills from a gambler. Sure, he turned in the money and blew the whistle on the gambler. But what about that play allowing the Danton Buccaneers to score a touchdown? The fact that Lou did not buy the deal, the fact that he never shaved a point, the fact that he reported the incident, the fact that he did not keep the payment, all of these facts were bound to be buried in the wave of publicity.

The implications frightened Lou. He wanted to go down in the annals of Meridian Browns' football as one of the great linebackers. But would he be remembered, even more, as the player who skirted the edges of a gambling scandal?

Lou wanted to play professional football. But could the pro teams afford a player with the taint of a gambler's deal, however innocent, in his college background?

He wanted to study law and practice law when his playing days came to an end. But where was a law school that wanted to enroll a student involved, however innocently, with illegal gambling interests?

The fear that others among his teammates might be involved became smaller and smaller in Lou's mind. Other fears, bigger ones, were overshadowing it. The need for Buck Foster to know became less and less compelling. Other needs were more important.

Lou wanted to talk with somebody about the problem —Paige, or Buck Foster, or Donny Campbell, or Brad Chapman. He briefly considered telephoning his father in Oklahoma. But he knew what all of them would tell him: hand over the money and tell the story right now. And Lou was sure that doing so would be the beginning of the end for his world.

He could not escape the thought.

Lou fingered the envelope in his jacket pocket as he walked through the field-house lobby, gray in the early morning light, and turned down the staircase toward the screening room in the basement.

The corridor of the basement was brightly lit. The aroma of brewing coffee drifted out of the screening room into the corridor. The odor had become a part of Lou's Sunday-morning routine. Lou heard the voices of the coaches as he approached the door to the screening room.

Foster looked up, frowning, when Lou entered. The head coach was seated at a small table, two assistant coaches standing over him. Foster was making marks on a yellow pad. The discussion of the previous day's game was getting started even before the film rolled. A student manager was threading the film into the projector.

Lou nodded a greeting to the coaches and dropped into a chair alongside Jackie Manteno, the only other player in the room. He kept his hand on the envelope in his jacket pocket.

Brad Chapman walked in. "Am I late?"

"Just getting started," Foster said. He nodded at the student manager. "Okay, let's go."

Brad took a seat behind Lou and Jackie.

48

The lights in the room went down. The film started to roll—forward, then backward for a second look and a comment, then forward again. Racing figures were running the ball, tackling, passing, blocking.

But none of the action registered on Lou. He sat, fingers on the envelope in his pocket, staring at the screen, unseeing.

Buck Foster's dry voice brought Lou's thoughts back to the game late in the first quarter. "See that, Powers?"

Lou focused his gaze on the screen. He saw himself chasing to his right after a Danton ballcarrier. Then he saw the ball in the air. He saw himself screeching to a halt, reversing himself, and beginning the futile race to prevent a touchdown.

"You committed yourself too quickly. With any other team, you'd have been all right. You would have smothered the play. But with a team like Danton, you've got to wait and watch. You've got to be sure—*sure*—you know where the play is going. A team like Danton has always got one more trick in the bag. You forgot that, and you got whipped. It cost a touchdown."

Coming from Foster, the statement almost amounted to an acknowledgment that Lou's error was understandable.

"Right," Lou said, and he settled back into his thoughts.

Lou wondered what Foster would have to say about the error if he knew that his middle linebacker was sitting here in the screening room holding $500, the gift of a gambler, in his pocket. The thought brought with it a decision: No, he would not tell Foster about the money and the man who gave it to him.

The money was there in his pocket. He could hand it over to Foster. He could tell the coach what had happened. That might be the right course. He had brought the money with him, after the long sleepless night, in case he decided to go to Foster with the problem.

But, no, he was not going to tell Foster or anyone. He knew now what he was going to do. His thoughts were tumbling forward, suddenly setting a strategy, mapping a way out of the mess. The chips were falling in place. What to do was simple, really.

The gambler is bound to contact me. I will meet with him. I will tell him it's no deal. I will give him the money back. I will leave and never see him again. Who's to know? Who will ever find out? For sure, the gambler never will tell. And, for sure, I will never tell.

Neat. Simple. Foolproof.

1

Lou's sense of relief was short-lived.

The game film was in the fourth quarter. The Browns were on top by a 21–7 score. They were driving for another touchdown. The Browns' forward wall was handling the Buccaneers with ease. Bull Hoffman was battering through the holes opened by the linemen for huge chunks of yardage. Donny Campbell, running behind Dave Emerson's blocking, was scampering around the ends, picking up five and six yards on every gallop.

Then Jackie Manteno took the snap from center, faked a hand-off to Bull, hid the ball on his hip, and rolled backward to pass. The Browns' line held. Jackie had all the time he needed.

Spider Willard was coming across the center of the field, ten yards deep, waving a hand above his head, calling for the pass. He was in the clear. Downfield, Donny Campbell was racing along the sideline toward the goal.

Jackie glanced at the scene, cocked his arm, and fired the ball—straight into the hands of a surprised Danton defensive halfback.

The halfback, startled, juggled the ball a moment. There were no Browns within ten yards—not Spider, not Donny, not anyone. The Buccaneer finally recovered and got a grip on the ball. He started running.

Spider, continuing his pattern across the field, veered toward the Danton halfback. He caught him and smashed him to the ground after a five-yard gain. The Meridian drive, which seemed sure of piling on another touchdown, was dead.

Lou blinked at the screen. He had seen the play when it occurred. He had been standing at the sideline with the other members of the defense, cheering the Browns' march to the goal. He had moaned in disappointment at the interception. It was a heartbreaker. But the best of quarterbacks will get intercepted on occasion, and Jackie Manteno had been intercepted—nothing more.

Lou and his defense took the field and held the Buccaneers, forcing them to punt the ball away. The interception turned out to be only a statistic in the record books. The game was won anyway. Nothing was changed by the interception. The extra touchdown would have provided sweet frosting on the cake for the Browns, but it was not needed. The interception did not matter.

But now, sitting in the screening room, touching the envelope in his jacket pocket, Lou felt a sense of horror.

A feeling of sickness, approaching nausea, swept over him.

"Roll it back," Buck Foster said.

The student manager had already stopped the projector. He had shown enough game films to know when the coaches wanted a second look. The figures on the screen danced jerkily backward to the point where Jackie brought the ball up to pass.

"Manteno, how in the hell do you explain that?" The voice was that of Bernie Carlisle, the backfield coach. "Tell me, how in the hell do you explain that?"

For a moment, the only sound in the room was the whirring of the projector, now flashing the pictures of Jackie bringing his arm forward and throwing the ball to a startled Danton player.

"My hand slipped, I guess," Jackie said softly.

The subdued tone did not fit the brash freshman, always cocky, a little too loud, sometimes downright hostile at the first hint of criticism.

"Your hand should slip on every pass," Carlisle said. "It was a perfect pass . . . only it went to a member of the other team."

Jackie said nothing.

The rerun proved the perfection of the pass: a rifle-shot spiral straight to the astonished Danton defender.

Lou glanced sideways at Jackie in the dim light of the screening room. He could hear in his mind the voice of the sad-eyed man in the trenchcoat: "I say Meridian by a couple of touchdowns, but no more—closer than most people figure." A couple of touchdowns—two touchdowns—a score of 21–7 on the scoreboard and no more.

Lou turned toward Jackie. He felt an angry urge to grab Jackie and shake him.

Jackie returned Lou's gaze with a quick glance, then turned back to the front. The quarterback's face revealed nothing.

Behind him, Lou heard Brad Chapman shift himself in his chair. As a quarterback, Brad Chapman understood full well the criticism aimed at Jackie. Brad had suffered the same on occasion in the past.

"It just didn't go where I fired it," Jackie said. Again, there was the subdued tone, so unlike Jackie. There was no trace of barely held anger, no hint of irritation about to explode. "That's all there is to it," Jackie added.

"Were you confused?" Foster asked.

"What?"

"Were you mixed up on the patterns your receivers were running?"

Lou knew that a quarterback, throwing at a spot, could come up looking silly on occasion. If a receiver broke a pattern, then he was not at the prescribed place when the ball arrived. If a quarterback threw to the wrong spot for whatever reason, then there was no receiver to catch the ball. Such miscues do occur. But seldom does a ball go on a perfect spiral straight into the arms of a defender for such an easy interception.

"I know the plays," Jackie said.

Foster let the matter drop, and the film rolled on to the end.

Leaving the field house, Brad turned toward his fraternity house. Lou and Jackie fell into step for the walk across the brick courtyard, Lou heading for the Sigma Chi house and Jackie going to his dormitory. All three were ready for the late breakfast that awaited them.

The courtyard, deserted in the gray morning when Lou had arrived at six o'clock, was now dotted with students. They were mostly in pairs, on their way to church services or, as the books under their arms indicated, going to the library to study.

As he and Jackie walked along, Lou struggled to find the right words for what he wanted to say. He could not open up with: "Say, I've been meaning to tell you, this strange-looking man gave me five hundred dollars, and I think he wants me to shave points in our games. Has he given you any money?" He could not blurt out: "Are you on the take?"

Jackie was the one who broke the silence. "What's with you, Mr. Big?" His voice was no longer the subdued monotone of the screening room. It was close to a snarl. "Are you the new quarterback coach or something?"

Stunned, Lou looked at the quarterback. He was not surprised that Jackie was upset by a tongue-lashing from Bernie Carlisle. Jackie had shown that he was thin-skinned plenty of times in the few weeks since he had come to Meridian. The ego that fueled his unmistakable star quality tolerated no criticism from others. Jackie maintained high quarterbacking standards for himself. He suffered when he fell short of his standards. His own harsh criticism of himself was sufficient in his view, so he did not like criticism from others. He had held his temper with the coaches, but he was not holding it now.

"What?" Lou said.

"You heard me."

"I heard you, but I don't know what you're talking about."

Jackie stopped walking and turned and faced Lou. The quarterback was almost a head shorter than Lou. He turned his angry face upward as he spoke. "I expected to get chewed out by Carlisle," he said. "That's Carlisle's job, to chew out players making errors. He had to say something, and he did say something." Jackie was spitting the words out with machine-gun speed. "But you—I don't have to take anything from you."

"I didn't chew you out. I didn't say anything."

"I saw the way you looked at me."

Lou started to voice his suspicion: "I think I know why you threw that interception. I think you were stopping the touchdown drive on purpose. I think you did it to preserve the point spread. I think you did it to hold our margin to two touchdowns." But he said nothing.

Jackie turned abruptly and walked away. He headed in the direction of his dormitory.

Lou stared at Jackie's back for a moment. Then he walked on toward the Sigma Chi house, frowning.

8

For Lou, the rest of Sunday was a wrestling match with his conscience, performed before an increasingly irritated Paige Hemphill.

"Something is wrong," Paige persisted. "Something has happened. And you should tell me about it."

They were strolling, hand in hand, across the campus. They walked slowly in a Sunday ritual of almost three years standing with them. Sunday afternoon, whether in sunshine or rain, in warm weather or cold—even in snow and ice—found Lou and Paige walking the campus, hand in hand. They walked and they talked. They spoke of living in cities with professional football teams. Lou liked the idea of Dallas, close to his Oklahoma homeland. Paige preferred Chicago, where she had grown up the daughter of a Chicago Bears' fan. They laughed and agreed they would probably wind up in Philadelphia or Los Angeles. They spoke of law schools for Lou. They talked about Paige continuing her sociology studies, going for an advanced degree. They talked about houses and apartments, furniture and cars. They walked and talked the Sunday afternoons away, winding up with dinner at the Brown House. Then they went home early for the start of another week.

But on this Sunday there had been little talk about any of those things, and no laughter. Lou was silent with his thoughts. He replied to Paige when he had to. Then he settled back into brooding about a stack of twenty-dollar bills, a man wearing a beige trenchcoat, and pass interceptions.

"What makes you think something is wrong?" Lou asked. He was stalling, trying to find an answer that would satisfy her. "Why do you say that something has happened?"

"I saw it in your face yesterday when you came out of the dressing room after the game. You looked worried then, almost distracted. Why was that? The Browns won the game. You won the game ball. What could possibly have been worrying you at that moment? And then, last night at the party, something was wrong. And now, today, it's the same."

For a moment, Lou was tempted to tell Paige the story: the first chance meeting with the man on the campus, the unexpected encounter after the Danton

58

game, the manila envelope, the money inside, his realization of what it all meant, his decision not to tell Buck Foster, his plan for extricating himself from the mess. Instead, he said, "It's nothing." He tried to smile. "You're seeing ghosts."

It would be good, Lou knew, to tell someone, to share the problem, to talk it out, to hear advice. He could trust Paige. He had no doubt of that. She would keep his confidence.

But her first statement would be, "Do you mean to say that you've still got the money!" Her second would be, "You've got to go to Buck Foster right now, give him the money, and tell him what has happened."

And then when Lou explained the implications—the suspicions that were bound to surround him, and the tarnishing spotlight of bad publicity—Paige was sure to say, "You've done nothing wrong. There is nothing for you to be worried about."

Lou knew that he would have no answers for Paige's arguments. She would be right, of course, on every count. Lou should not still have the money in his possession. He knew it. Lou, of course, should have told Buck Foster about the incident immediately. He knew it. And Lou should, he knew, have nothing to fear. Beyond question, Paige would be right.

But still there was a chance, a hope that he could extricate himself—quietly, secretly, with no one the wiser, ever. He had a plan: meet the gambler, return the money, reject the deal. He would be out of the mess, free of it, with no blot on his reputation, no questions about his honesty, no bright glare of the public spotlight. The plan would work. It had to work.

Paige would say, "You're wrong."

Lou could only reply, "You don't understand." So he said nothing to Paige about the incident.

Besides, now there was more involved than Lou Powers. Now there was the added specter of Jackie Manteno's throwing an interception on purpose to protect a gambler's point spread. Lou knew what Paige would say, too, about his suspicions of Jackie: "Ridiculous! Now who's seeing ghosts?"

Maybe so, thought Lou. Perhaps the possibility that a freshman quarterback with a brilliant future at Meridian and then a brilliant future in professional football would risk everything, along with his honor, for a few dollars handed over by a gambler was ridiculous.

In truth, Jackie's outburst while they were standing on the brick courtyard in front of the field house seemed to Lou to be an encouraging sign. His reaction was not that of a man who intentionally threw an interception, not the response of a guilty man. Rather, it was the usual Jackie Manteno shooting-from-the-hip reply to the first hint of criticism from the outside.

But the coincidences were too many to shrug off. Lou frowned and walked silently with Paige as he counted the coincidences in his mind. Fact: a gambler had made an overture to a Meridian Brown player, linebacker Lou Powers. Fact: the gambler predicted a two-touchdown point spread in Meridian's victory over the Danton Buccaneers. Fact: Jackie Manteno's interception killed a Meridian drive and preserved the two-touchdown point spread. Fact: if the gambler wanted to buy the services of the leader of the defense, he surely would want to buy the services of the leader of the Browns' offense, too. And, fact: Jackie Manteno, as the quarterback, was the leader of the Browns' offense.

The weight of the evidence against Jackie led Lou into reconsidering his decision not to go to Buck Foster with his facts and his suspicions. But he could not do so without revealing his own contact with the gambler. He would have to reveal that he was holding $500 handed to him by the gambler.

Once again, briefly, the thought returned that he could wash his hands of the whole mess in one fell swoop by telling the coach and turning over the money. But he knew it simply was not so. The publicity and the resulting suspicions would stain his record and cloud his future. No doubt about it.

There had to be another way. There was. He had his plan now. He would stick to it. Besides, going to Buck Foster with his suspicions of Jackie would mean charging a teammate with shaving points for a payoff from a gambler, a serious charge. And based on what? One pass interception. Nothing more. No, Lou was sure of his course now.

By the time Lou and Paige ended their walk and arrived at the Brown House for dinner, he knew that he

61

was not going to say anything to anyone. He was more certain than ever that his decision was the right one. His plan, when studied from every angle, appeared perfect. There were no holes. It was going to work. The episode was going to end as quickly as it had started. Soon the man and his money would seem as though they never had entered Lou Powers' life. As for Jackie or anyone else on the team, for that matter, Lou resolved to watch and wait. There was no other route for him to take.

The feeling that the decision was made freed Lou's mind during dinner. He enjoyed himself, for the first time in more than twenty-four hours. Sitting beneath the portraits of Meridian's all-American football players, himself included, he felt at home and relaxed with Paige.

But Paige still had not had her questions answered. As they walked back to her dormitory, she told Lou, "Maybe we shouldn't see so much of each other."

"What do you mean?"

"Maybe we should see less of each other for a while. It might be good . . . the best thing . . . for both of us."

"Why?"

"Oh, we're together almost all the time—almost all of your free time—and maybe it would be better—for both of us, you know—if we were not together all the time."

Lou was grateful for the arrival of Monday morning. He would return to the routine of the classroom. The instructors would require him to think about something besides the sad-eyed man wearing a beige trenchcoat. He would return to the football field. The demands of the coaches and the collisions of the game would keep his mind off the packet of twenty-dollar bills tucked away in his bureau drawer.

Too, the activities of the weekday routine would remove him from the questioning gaze of Paige Hemphill. Her unerring instinct that something was wrong bothered him. It bothered him more than her suggestion that they see less of each other for a while. She had not meant that. Lou was sure of it. She was miffed at the time by his moody behavior. She would forget she had said it.

A slight drizzle was beginning to fall—a signal of colder weather on the way—when Lou stepped out of the front door of the Sigma Chi house and turned toward the campus. For a moment he considered returning to his room and exchanging his windbreaker jacket for a raincoat. Then he shrugged and walked on. The rain was barely more than a mist.

By the time Lou reached the campus the misty drizzle was ending. He turned the corner around the red-brick business administration building and took the last few steps toward the front door. He stepped inside and looked around the lobby, crowded with milling students.

Paige had a class at the same time in the same building. They met here every Monday, Wednesday, and Friday for a brief greeting before heading their separate ways.

"You look lost." Donny Campbell was standing in front of Lou, smiling.

"Have you seen Paige here this morning?"

A bell rang, calling the students to their classes.

"Yeah, she was going into a classroom down there," Donny said, gesturing to his right.

"Oh."

9

Lou spotted the sad-eyed man in the beige trenchcoat, standing in the crowd alongside the practice field.

The Browns were engaged in a Wednesday ritual, the first-team offense versus the first-team defense in full-speed scrimmage. This one was special, and the crowd of fans jamming the sidelines was even larger than usual for a Browns' practice session. Up on the eight-foot-high platform where Coach Buck Foster watched his Browns in practice, and all over the field, television cameramen recorded the action from a dozen different angles. The Browns were being videotaped in practice for a television network special.

Riding atop the national polls, and with a rich football tradition dating back more than five decades, the Browns were a natural.

"Don't pay any attention to them," Foster told the players. "Don't let them bother you. It's no different, really, from a televised game."

With a middle linebacker named Lou Powers being mentioned prominently for the Heisman Trophy, and a sensational freshman quarterback named Jackie Manteno heading for the all-American teams, the title of the television special was a natural, too: "The Best Ever."

"That's their title, not mine," was Foster's acid comment. "This team has eight more games to play before anyone can call us the best ever."

Lou and the players knew why Foster, always all business when it came to football, allowed the extraordinary intrusion in the Browns' practice session. There were two reasons. First, television exposure was sure to pay off during the recruiting season next spring. All over the country, standout high-school players were sure to watch the television special. The show might influence one, two, or a dozen to choose Meridian for their college football careers. Foster had another reason, too. The voters in the weekly polls—the writers and broadcasters for the AP, the coaches for the UPI—were sure to be watching. The image of greatness portrayed on the television screen would not be lost on those deciding the national championship.

The cameramen and the producers had been in the dressing room before practice while the players were changing clothes. They were escorted by Scotty Hanks, the Browns' publicity director, who pointed out players by name and suggested shots he thought might be useful.

66

Now the cameramen and the producers were everywhere on the field with their minicam units, taping each minute of the play from all angles.

Lou was getting to his feet after stopping a plunge through the middle of the line. He turned his back to the line of scrimmage to set up the huddle and call the defensive signals for the next play. Idly his eyes passed over the spectators at the sideline. The slight figure with the sad expression and the fixed smile seemed to jump out of the crowd at him. Normally, the crowds at the Browns' practice sessions were nothing more than a blur to Lou. He was only vaguely aware of their presence. Yet the figure of the little man stood out clearly against the background of the others in the crowd. The man was watching Lou. Their eyes met for a moment. The man gave a barely perceptible nod, as if acknowledging a greeting.

Lou drew his defensive crew around him. "Let's go," he said absently, clapping his hands together to command attention. The picture of the man's face remained in Lou's mind. "Let's go," he repeated. "Hear me now."

Otis Hildegard, the defense coach, leaned into the crowd of players around Lou. Hildegard always listened, without comment, to Lou's defensive plan for the next play.

A cameraman knelt between two players opposite Lou in the huddle, pointing his lens at Lou's face.

"Let's shoot the gap on them, just for fun," Lou said. "We'll see what they do when they're surprised."

Seldom did Lou feel a need to call a defensive play

sending himself charging from his middle linebacker post through the line in pursuit of the ballcarrier. The sturdy front four of the Browns' defense, the two tackles and two guards, were strong rushers. They bulldozed their way into the offensive backfield with regularity. Quarterbacks trying to pass and runners trying to get up steam bit the dust in a losing effort with startling frequency. The strength of the front four left Lou free to roam the linebackers' corridor, ready to knock down a pass or move up to help stop a running play.

Hildegard nodded unconsciously at Lou's signal and stepped back. The cameraman scampered back to the sideline, out of the area of upcoming collision.

The offense was approaching the line of scrimmage. The center, Steve Sherman, bent over the ball. The linemen dropped into their stance.

Jackie Manteno walked up behind Sherman. He was looking beyond the center, at Lou. He was trying to guess what the middle linebacker, poised four yards behind the line of scrimmage, directly in front of the quarterback, was planning.

Leaning slightly forward, arms hanging loose at his sides, Lou returned Jackie's stare. He gave no sign of his intentions.

Jackie barked the quarterback signals, took the snap, and stepped back with the ball, turning as he went.

Lou leaped forward. Plunging between the guards, he caught Steve Sherman by surprise. With both hands, Lou shoved the off-balance center to his right. A half step farther in, Lou heaved a shoulder into an unsuspecting lineman and crashed into the backfield at full speed.

Jackie was completing his turn and extending the ball to the waiting hands of Dave Emerson. Lou blasted into them. Jackie, Dave, and the ball bounced in different directions.

The hulking form of Mike Rushman, charging forward from his tackle position, moved past Lou in a blur and covered the loose football for a fumble recovery.

The cheers roared in from the sideline.

The cameramen turned their aim from the playing field to the leaping, shouting students on the sideline. In the tradition of great defenses, this play was the Meridian Browns' style of football.

Lou was smiling when he got to his feet. The play felt good. The defense had whipped the offense, out-smarting them with Lou's play call and beating them physically.

Jackie Manteno was smiling, too, as he slapped Lou on the shoulder pads. "Beautiful," Jackie said.

The accolade was no surprise to Lou. Jackie's anger of Sunday morning had, as always, faded as quickly as it had flared. To Jackie Manteno, each day was a new beginning. There was no yesterday. Nor was Lou sur-prised that the quarterback seemed pleased at being knocked to the ground and having his play busted. Jackie did not enjoy it, to be sure, but he had good reason to applaud the play. In a game, Lou's devastating charge, forcing a fumble by an opponent, meant ball possession for Jackie's offense and the chance to score.

The thought put a frown on Lou's face. He remembered a similar linebacker blitz in the Danton game that shook loose a fumble. The Browns took possession and started the drive in the fourth quarter that ended with Jackie's pass interception.

Unconsciously Lou turned and glanced at the sideline. The man in the beige trenchcoat was still watching him. The sad-eyed smile was fixed in place. The man nodded slightly to Lou again.

The grinding scrimmage lasted until the sun, quite low, cast long shadows on the field. With the end of the afternoon, the autumn breeze was nippy. The sideline lookers were drifting away, their coat collars turned up against the chill.

Lou galloped through the wind sprints ending the drills, up and down the field, with the cameramen following him all the way with their lenses. Coming off the field, Lou angled away from the procession of players strung out down the gently sloping hill toward the dressing room in the field house.

The television crews were moving off the practice field too, heading for the dressing room for more shots. The man in the beige trenchcoat was moving out toward Lou. Others in the dwindling crowd of spectators—friends and fans—were moving in the same direction as the man, walking toward players they knew for a final word at the end of the practice.

"Good practice," the man said, when he and Lou met.

"I've got to see you," Lou said.

The man smiled without speaking. Then, ignoring Lou's statement, he said, "The Lewiston Panthers are

70

terrible this year. The spread hit twenty-eight points today. Twenty-eight! The smart people are saying that you will win by much more—maybe thirty-five or even forty-two points. But I think there are going to be some surprised people. I'm figuring Lewiston is laying for you. You'll beat them, of course, but I figure only by about fifteen points. Maybe more than two touchdowns, but less than three touchdowns." He paused. "What do you think?"

Lou felt a sudden moment of terror. He looked around. Nobody was paying attention to his conversation. Most of the players were moving toward the field house. The few still engaged in a moment's chatter at the sideline were several yards away. They were intent on their own conversation. Besides, Lou Powers being accosted by a stranger for a few moments of conversation was nothing new to anyone.

"I've got to see you," Lou repeated. "A meeting. We've got to talk."

The man frowned briefly at the suggestion. Then the frown vanished. The sad-eyed smile was back in place. "Oh, I see," he said, speaking as if he had solved a puzzle. "It's fifteen hundred dollars a game, if that is what you were wondering about. You didn't think it was just five hundred dollars, did you?"

Lou flushed. The man was certain he had bought Lou Powers.

Lou had to have a private meeting to return the money to the man. He knew where he wanted the meeting—a place where they could sit down, with a table

71

between them so Lou could lay out the money, a place Lou could walk away from, perhaps escaping unrecognized: the Blue Moon truck stop on the edge of Meridian. The customers, for the most part, were truckers passing through on the interstate highway. The Meridian students never went there. Few townspeople frequented the out-of-the-way spot. It was perfect.

"I can find the place," the man said. "But why?"

Lou took a deep breath. "You don't think I'm going to get into something like this without getting a few things ironed out, do you? We can't stand here and talk forever."

The man stared at Lou for a moment without speaking. Finally he said, "Okay, nine o'clock."

Lou jogged down the hill toward the field house.

10

Lou's hands were sweating when he steered the car he had borrowed at the Sigma Chi house into the Blue Moon parking lot.

The time was 8:55.

The parking lot, well-lit around the gas pumps in front, was crowded at the side with the huge eighteen-wheel rigs from the interstate highway.

Lou found a parking place in a row of cars at the side of the building and pulled in.

Walking toward the door, he kept both hands in his jacket pockets. His hands were shaking. In the right hand he held tightly to the white envelope containing the stack of twenty-dollar bills. Carefully sealed, it made a compact package, easily handed over. In the envelope

73

the money was hidden from the casual glance of a waitress or a customer walking by.

At the door, Lou stopped a moment, took a deep breath, and pulled the door open. Inside, he scanned the crowd quickly. The sad-eyed man with the fixed smile was not there yet.

But Lou was not only checking for the man he was meeting. He glanced around the large room, searching the faces for any signs of recognition. The counter was filled with people. No familiar faces there. A roped-off area in the corner bore the sign: *Fast Service for Truckers Only*. It was half-filled. Little danger of recognition from that corner. He looked around at the other booths and tables—truckers, families on a trip stopping for hamburgers and coffee, a group of high-school boys sipping soft drinks. Lou studied the boys, who probably were local. He did not recognize any of them, but they might recognize him. He had attended high-school football letterman banquets in the area with the Meridian coaches for four years. The boys did not look up at Lou as he slid into a booth.

For a frightening moment Lou was sure that everyone in the place was looking at him. He wished his face had not been on the cover of *Sports Illustrated* magazine the week before. Even a trucker on his way from Minneapolis to Atlanta might recognize him. Someone might walk in carrying a copy of the magazine. Someone might walk up to him at any minute with the familiar question: "Say, aren't you . . . ?"

74

Suddenly the sad-eyed man was across the table from Lou in the booth.

Lou involuntarily jumped slightly. "You startled me," he said.

The man's small, fixed smile was in place. "All right," he said pleasantly, "what's on your mind?"

A waitress, used to giving fast service, appeared. "Are you ready to order?"

The man looked up. "Just coffee, please."

"Coke," Lou said.

She went away.

"What's on your mind?" the man repeated.

Lou kept his hands in his jacket pockets. He did not think his hands were shaking now. But they might start.

"Are any other members of the team in on this deal?"

The man's face showed nothing. "That is none of your business," he said quietly. "Same as it's nobody else's business that you're in on the deal."

Lou looked at the man. He felt the envelope containing the currency in his pocket.

"We didn't meet for you to ask that, did we?"

"No," Lou said, taking a deep breath. While driving to the Blue Moon he had rehearsed the words he was going to say. He began speaking. "I don't buy the deal. I did not ask for the deal—I don't know why you picked me—and I'm not going to do what you want. We are meeting for me to tell you that and to give you your money back."

Lou pulled the envelope out of his pocket. His hand

75

was not shaking. He laid the envelope on the table in front of the man. "There it is, all of it." Lou said. "I don't want it."

The man looked at the envelope. But he made no move toward it and said nothing. Then he reached out with a forefinger and slid the envelope full of currency to his left, toward the inside edge of the booth. He lifted a small cardboard tent advertising triple-decker Moon Burgers and placed it over the envelope.

Lou was frightened. Something in the man's manner was alarming. But there was nothing to fear from him —not seated here in the Blue Moon with crowds of people all around. What was there to be afraid of? But Lou's breath was coming fast. He knew why he was frightened. His plan, so perfect in his thoughts, was now all he had. He was committed to it. There was no going back, no room for revision now.

Finally the man spoke. "Isn't it enough?" he asked.

"What do you mean?"

"You want more? The price is not high enough?"

Lou felt a flash of anger. The man was convinced Lou Powers could be bought. The only question was price.

"I thought I made myself clear," Lou said. He realized his voice was trembling slightly. "I don't buy the deal. Understand?"

Lou and the man stared at each other across the table for a brief moment.

"Now, I'm going to leave. And if you ever approach me again, I'll go straight to the police." He started to slide out of the booth.

"Wait."

Lou stopped.

The waitress arrived with the coffee and the Coke.

Lou slid back into the booth. He did not want to. He knew he should have kept on going and walked out. But the one-word command had carried the alarming tone of a threat.

"One thing, and then, no hard feelings," the man said. "A bit of advice."

"What?"

The man took a sip of his coffee and leaned back in the booth. The smile left his face. "Listen to me," he said softly, "and let us have no misunderstanding. You will regret it—deeply regret it—if you discuss this with anyone. I assume that you have not, so far. Your threat to go to the police if I approach you again seems ample evidence you've kept this to yourself so far. If you're smart, you'll keep it that way—to yourself. My associates and I are not playing kiddie games. You are in the real world, like it or not. You can decide to pass up the dough—stupidly—and that's your business. But don't be stupid enough to talk to the police, the coaches, the papers—anybody. You could wind up with a broken leg."

Lou felt his jaw muscles tighten. His anger returned and welled up inside of him. He wanted, more than anything at that moment, to grab the man's necktie with his left hand and smash the man's face with his right fist.

The man did not seem worried. "Understand?" he asked. The sad-eyed smile was back in place.

"I heard you," Lou said.

"It could happen anyway, you know. People have accidents. If you're not with us, you're against us. So be careful."

Lou glared at the man for a moment. Then he got up and walked out.

11

The sunshine was bright and unseasonably hot for an autumn day in Pennsylvania when the Browns took the field for their game with the Lewiston Panthers.

All around the stadium, fans were peeling off coats and sweaters and folding them in their laps. Later, when the sun was setting in the late afternoon, the garments might feel good. But not now.

The stadium was packed. Many of the fans wore the bright blue of the Lewiston Panthers and waved their blue pennants in support of the team.

At the twenty-yard line on the western side of the stadium, the small crowd of Meridian fans stood out in the traditional brown. They were a happy bunch. With the runaway victory over Norring Tech and the decisive triumph over the tough Danton Buccaneers, the Browns were riding high. They were proving the preseason polls to be correct. The Browns this year were probably headed for an undefeated season and the national championship. The fans were feeling confident and enjoying it.

The Lewiston Panthers, on the other hand, were stumbling through a dreadful season, their worst in many years. Usually they were one of the giants of college football. Their high standing, year in and year out, rated them a place on the Browns' schedule. Battles between the Browns and the Panthers had shaken the football world, and more than once in the past the national championship had ridden on the outcome of the game between them. But this year the Panthers, weakened by graduation and hampered by a rash of preseason practice injuries, were falling on bad days. Not only had they lost their first two games, they had been beaten soundly. They showed an impotent offense and an inadequate defense. Worse yet for the Panthers, neither of the teams that walloped them so badly was anywhere near the measure of the Meridian Browns.

Clearly, a rout of major proportions was in the making. Doubtless, the Panthers were going to be the easiest game of the season for the Browns.

A friend at the Sigma Chi house had wisecracked to Lou, "Why don't you ask for the weekend off? The Browns aren't going to need Lou Powers out there on the field this Saturday."

Lou had managed a smile at the remark, but he found little to smile about as the week wound down to a close. Scenes from the past week kept swirling through his mind. They were not pleasant scenes—not any of them.

Walking through Wier Cook Airport in Indianapolis to board the plane for Pennsylvania, Lou had caught himself looking around for the man with the sad-eyed smile. The little man was supposed to vanish from Lou's mind once the money had been returned. But now the money had been returned, and still the man's face was there. Lou could hear the soft voice repeating, "Meridian by two touchdowns over Danton," and now, "Meridian by less than three touchdowns over Lewiston." The man's face was always smiling when he spoke.

The unsmiling face that delivered a threat of physical violence was there in Lou's mind too. Physical fear had no place in Lou Powers' makeup. But the movies he had seen and the books he had read about the gangster element worked on his imagination. He did not doubt that talking could lead to trouble. He knew, too, that there was such a thing as "teaching a lesson to others," which could mean trouble for him whether he talked or not.

Paige Hemphill was even cooler now, and with reason. Her brightly smiling face, with eyes that always seemed to sparkle, was serious, clouded, almost angry. She had tried to telephone Lou shortly after eight o'clock on Wednesday evening. Lou was not at the Sigma Chi house. He was out. Where? Nobody at the Sigma Chi house seemed to know.

"Didn't you get my message?" Paige asked the next morning.

"Yes, but it was late. I thought you probably were in bed."

"Where were you?" She was neither prying nor nagging. She was simply asking, as Lou might have asked if their roles had been reversed. "They said you had borrowed a car, but nobody knew where you had gone."

"I had to meet a person," Lou said. He added quickly, "A man." He paused. "It was a business matter."

Paige waited. Then she said, "Oh."

At noon Friday she was not at the send-off rally when the team boarded buses for the short ride to the Indianapolis airport and the flight to Pennsylvania. She needed to put in the time in the library on a research project, she said.

The face of Jackie Manteno, too, would not leave Lou's mind. He wasn't bothered by the face of the quarterback snapping at Lou while they stood on the courtyard in front of the field house on Sunday morning. Lou had seen the famous Manteno temper in action before. The picture that would not leave Lou's mind was of the quarterback's face while he was explaining the pass interception. Jackie's expression as he glanced at Lou revealed that he had recognized Lou's shock. There were no words. But the message had been exchanged when their eyes met. Lou was afraid of what it might mean.

There were other faces in Lou's mind: Bull Hoffman, Donny Campbell, Spider Willard. Had any of them, or all of them, spoken to the sad-eyed little man? Had they bought the deal?

Now, going through the warm-up calisthenics in the hot autumn sunshine, Lou tried to shake the troublesome faces—all of them—out of his mind. He tried to concentrate on the mental exercise, "psyching up," that was every bit as important to greatness on the football field as loosening up the body. But he was not succeeding.

The Browns had not had a good week on the practice field. They had been a free and easy bunch, almost rollicking, as they moved through the week. They knew the Lewiston Panthers' record. They knew the troubles the Panthers were having trying to put together an effective offense and a solid defense. The Lewiston Panthers were going to present the lightest threat the Browns would face all season. The Browns reacted to the knowledge with something akin to a holiday spirit. Loose, relaxed, unworried, they enjoyed the practice week.

The network television crew had been a distraction, to be sure, but the problem was greater than that. Lou knew the problem: overconfidence. Not once during the practice week had the Browns exhibited the intensity, the grueling drive, the serious concentration that marked the practice-field work of a great football team.

Buck Foster and the assistant coaches drove the players increasingly hard. They were determined to hold down the growing feeling that the Lewiston Panthers were offering nothing more than a cakewalk ball game. But obviously nobody on the team was worried. The game was going to be a field day, a runaway, a massacre. It was going to be fun.

12

The Browns won the coin toss. But from there, everything went wrong.

The Panthers' opening kickoff backed Donny Campbell up to the goal line. Donny gathered in the ball, faked a start to his left, then swept to his right. He was heading for the sideline behind the charging form of Dave Emerson. Out of nowhere, a Lewiston tackler knifed through and slammed into Donny at the ten-yard line. Donny kept his balance and spun, trying to break free. Then another Lewiston tackler crashed in. Donny went down—and the ball went up.

The loose ball bounded lazily backward, toward the goal line. Dave, seeing what had happened, skidded to a halt, turned, and raced toward the loose ball. But the second Lewiston tackler, feeling or seeing the ball break away from Donny's grasp, was scrambling over Donny's fallen form toward the ball. He outdistanced Dave easily and pounced on the fumble at the four-yard line.

Another Lewiston player, and then Dave, hit the pile, but the Lewiston player gripping the ball held on, snuggling the ball against his stomach. The other Lewiston players, charging toward the action, mobbed their teammate, who was on his feet now, dancing a jig, holding the ball above his head in one hand.

All around the giant bowl of a stadium, the Lewiston fans were on their feet cheering.

On the sideline, the Browns stood motionless, dazed by what had happened. The fumble itself was bad news. Even if the Browns had recovered the loose ball, they were left with their backs to the wall, deep in their own territory, to start their first drive. Then bad turned to worse. Lewiston recovered the fumble.

On the field, the Browns were throwing their blocks, unaware of what was happening behind them. Then they got to their feet and turned, puzzled, to stare at the wild jubilation of the Panthers at the end of the field. Suddenly they knew what had happened.

"Powers!"

Lou turned toward the sound of the voice.

Buck Foster was wearing the same unchanging frown on his face. He was not looking at Lou. He was staring at the scene on the field. Then he swung his arm in a wide arc gesturing Lou and his defensive unit onto the field.

The coach's shouted command had interrupted a disturbing thought halfway through Lou's mind. "Fifteen points. More than two touchdowns maybe, but less than three touchdowns."

Lou jogged onto the field to take up the defense at the four-yard line.

Donny passed him, eyes on the ground, on the way to the bench. The little speedster seldom fumbled. He had picked a bad place for this one. Behind Donny came Dave, his eyes also on the ground. Dave was generally acknowledged to be one of the best blocking backs in the country. He had picked a bad place to miss a block and let a tackler come slashing through.

Across the field, the excited Lewiston quarterback was leaning toward his coach at the sideline. He was getting the final shouted instruction before joining the huddle on the field. All around the Lewiston coach and his quarterback, the players at the sideline were leaping and shouting their greetings to the players coming off the field.

The Browns' defense was in place, ready for the goal-line stand, when the Lewiston quarterback came racing onto the field to join his huddle. Lou, standing on the goal line, four yards behind the line of scrimmage, watched the Panthers break the huddle and come out to take their positions.

Lou had no doubts about what was coming. The Panthers were an I-formation team. The I formation was perfectly suited for a short-yardage gainer at the goal line. Nothing was stronger than the I formation for handing off to a fullback leaping over the center of the line. Powerful and airborne, the fullback was virtually unstoppable in such a play. But Lou considered no runner, airborne or not, to be unstoppable. He had stopped the best of them, and he must stop this one.

Lou braced himself to meet the leaping charge at the middle of the line in a stand-up position. The collision of flying fullback and charging linebacker would be earthshaking.

The Panthers lined up in their I formation. Then, suddenly, the Panthers shifted. The quarterback dropped back into a tailback position, five yards behind the center. The fullback shifted into a position in front and just to the right of the quarterback, to provide protective blocking. The other two backs moved into flanker positions to the left.

Lou blinked at the formation in front of him. It appeared at first glance to be a variation of the shotgun offense used by the Dallas Cowboys on passing downs. But nothing like it ever had been mentioned during the week's practice. The Browns' coaches never mentioned the Lewiston Panthers might use the shotgun offense. Nobody knew the Panthers had the formation in their playbook. It was something new, designed and developed to surprise the Meridian Browns. The Panthers were pulling their surprise early, to try to cash in on the fumble recovery and mark up the game's first touchdown.

A moment's panic swept over Lou. He must decide what to do, but there was no time to think. In such uncertain moments, a linebacker must rely on the only weapon left in his arsenal: instinct. The ingrained knowledge built of a thousand tackles in previous games must call the shot. The experience was not new to Lou. Teams frequently—almost always, in fact—sprang special surprises on the Meridian Browns, a tribute, in a way, to the Browns' tradition of mighty defenses. Lou had had a lot of practice falling back on his instincts and had made his reputation as a premier linebacker by having the right instinct more often than not. But always there was the brief flash of panic when facing the unexpected. The panic seemed to trigger Lou's instincts.

Thoughts clicked through Lou's mind automatically. Clearly, the formation was designed for a pass. But where? To whom? The point of attack seemed loaded to the left of the Panthers' backfield, to Lou's right.

Lou glanced quickly to his right and left, at his partners in the linebacker slots. To his right, Marion Petoskey was bracing to bear the brunt of the receivers set to flood his area. To Lou's left, he noticed with alarm that Henry Alderman was edging in toward the center, taking the bait of the Panthers' lopsided backfield. That was stupid. Henry was leaving himself vulnerable to a block shoving him farther in toward the center. He could find himself knocked out of the play, and the Browns' defensive halfback would be left alone to protect the outside against a pass.

Lou started to shout and wave Henry back. But it was too late. The Lewiston center was snapping the ball on a low trajectory back to the quarterback.

Lou held his position, guarding his zone against the pass.

The quarterback took the snap just above the knees, brought the ball up, stepped to his left, and cocked his arm. He was looking to his left, where the two flanker backs were sifting into the end zone. Marion Petoskey was dropping back to help the outnumbered defensive halfback.

Lou resisted the temptation to move over in the direction of the quarterback's glance, to help shore up the defense in the area. The picture in the back of his mind of Henry being sucked out of position by the threat of the two flankers kept Lou in his center zone, watchful. Lou wondered, too, about the fullback. With the right end, he could flood the other side of the end zone.

The quarterback quickly changed his aim from the left to the right. The end was circling in the end zone. The fullback, having thrown one block, was drifting in the same direction. Henry, caught out of position, was on the ground, having given up a sharp blocking angle to a Lewiston tackle coming across.

Lou broke into a full-speed run to his left, where he was sure the pass was to go. The Browns' defensive halfback was covering the Panthers' right end in the corner of the end zone. Lou headed for the Panther fullback, who was making his turn in the area where Henry Alderman should have been.

The ball arrived before Lou did. Lou veered to avoid smashing into the fullback, now clutching the ball to his chest—touchdown.

The scoreboard flickered: Panthers 6, Visitors 0.

All around the stadium, the thousands of Lewiston

fans were on their feet shouting. Their Panthers, dismal failures in their first two games, heavy underdogs in this game, were in the lead.

The Panthers on the field were leaping gleefully around the fullback.

A few seconds later, Lou's leaping charge into the middle of the line failed to block the kick for the extra point. The scoreboard blinked again: Panthers 7, Visitors 0.

Lou watched Henry Alderman as the defensive unit walked off the field. Henry's face was a blank. Henry knew the touchdown had been scored in his zone. He knew he was on the ground when it happened. He knew he had been caught out of position. The knowledge of these facts was clear behind the dull stare on his face.

But Lou could not help thinking that any gambler wanting to control the point spread with one linebacker was bound to feel that two linebackers would be twice as good.

13

At the half time the score stood the same: 7–0.

Following the lightning-quick touchdown in the opening minutes, the two teams had battled each other between the thirty-yard lines. Neither was able to break through with the big play on offense or defense that spelled score. The Panthers' offense, fired up by the gift touchdown, held the vaunted Meridian defense at bay. The Browns were unable to come up with one of their bombshell defensive plays so as to knock the Panthers back into a deep hole. At the same time, the Panthers' defense was having little trouble bottling up a lifeless Meridian attack. The Meridian offense was paying the price of joyful overconfidence during the practice week. They were functioning like a rusty machine.

Despite the reading on the scoreboard, the two teams

had in no way played evenly following the stunning Lewiston touchdown. True, neither team had added to the score. But the Panthers were playing the Browns off their feet.

The players on both sides knew it. At the sound of the gun ending the first half, the Panthers charged off the field, hands raised, acting for all the world as if they had already won the game. After all, they were leading the nation's top-ranked football team. They had held them for a half, and they needed only to hold them for another half. The Browns, at the other side of the field, trooped to their dressing room like a beaten team. They knew they were being outplayed.

In the dressing room, Lou sat slumped on a bench, leaning back against a locker. He was listening to Otis Hildegard, the defensive coach, lecture on the problems of the first half and the solutions for the second half.

But Lou's mind wandered as Hildegard droned on. Lou already knew the problems. He knew the Browns had gone into the game with an acute case of overconfidence. Everyone knew it. But Lou knew more. He knew that a nameless little man with a sad-eyed smile had tried to buy a point spread—and that Donny Campbell had fumbled, Dave Emerson had missed a key block, Henry Alderman had been lured out of position, and the Lewiston Panthers had scored. Lou knew, too, that Jackie Manteno's passes were not connecting, that Spider Willard dropped one he should have caught, that Bull Hoffman was being stopped cold at the line. The face of the sad-eyed man would not go away. Lou watched Hildegard without hearing what the coach was saying.

Buck Foster, glaring at everyone but saying nothing, moved from Hildegard's defensive crew to Bernie Carlisle and the offensive unit and back again to the defense, watching and listening.

Finally, at the end, Foster spoke. "You've made enough dumb mistakes in the first half to last the Meridian Browns for ten years. Football games are won by concentration and execution. You did not concentrate and you did not execute in the first half. You will in the second half, or you will lose this game."

For Lou, the dumb mistakes in the first half were just a beginning. Unconsciously, he strained to extend himself. He overreached his zone when the play was heading for Henry Alderman. He was fearful that Henry might misstep again. He began doing the same on Marion Petoskey's side of the field. The Browns could not afford a Petoskey misstep either. He charged through the line more often than was wise, trying to shore up the front four. Expecting a pass, he dropped back, more quickly and deeper than he should to cover for the defensive halfbacks. They, too, might misstep. His suspicions were eroding his confidence in his teammates, a fatal error for a middle linebacker and defensive captain.

Already he had been caught twice. On a run up the middle, Lou was angling to his left to cover a fake into Henry Alderman's territory. He was not there when the runner burst through the center of the line. On a blitz, he left his zone open for a short pass over center.

Lou brought himself up short. He knew the dangers. Soon the Lewiston Panthers would size up what was happening. The quarterback on the field or the spotter in the press box would notice the chink in the Browns' defensive armor. They would not understand what was happening, but they would know what they were seeing. Then it would be a simple matter to adjust the attack to take advantage of the situation. There would be more plays faking to the outside, luring Lou out of position, and then going straight up the middle. There would be more plays aimed at enticing Lou to blitz, with a short pass going over center into his vacant zone.

A chilling thought hit Lou. His own misplay, getting himself caught out of position, was precisely the stuff of which a point-spread bargain is made. It was the way a linebacker would deliver on a point-spread deal—and probably get away with it. If the sad-eyed man in the beige trenchcoat was up there somewhere in the stadium watching, he must be thinking that Lou Powers had changed his mind and bought the deal.

Lou lined up for the next play. He resolved to concentrate on his middle linebacker job. He would quit worrying about his teammates. He would let them handle their assignments, and he would handle his.

The third quarter was ticking away toward the end. Still the teams were battling between the thirty-yard lines. Neither team was able to put together anything resembling a sustained drive. Neither team was able to explode for a score or to stop the other cold and shove them back. The two teams rocked back and forth, the seconds ticking away, the score standing out on the scoreboard: Panthers 7, Visitors 0.

The Panthers stood now at the Browns' forty-seven-yard line, third down and six yards to go for a first down.

Lou, watching the Panthers break their huddle, expected them to line up in their shotgun formation, left unused since the first minute of the game. The down, the yardage, the field position, everything seemed to dictate a pass. The shotgun formation was made to order for the situation. If everyone knew that a pass was needed, and everyone knew that a pass was coming, and indeed there was going to be a pass, the shotgun formation was perfect. It provided no trickery, no deception, only a few valuable extra seconds for the quarterback scanning the field for a receiver. But the quarterback lined the Panthers up in their usual I formation. He barked the signals and took the snap.

Lou shifted slightly, watching, in his position four yards behind the line of scrimmage.

The quarterback whirled and raced back a half-dozen steps and set himself to throw. A flanker was circling out to Lou's right. Instinctively Lou moved slightly toward the right side of his zone. He glanced from the flanker to the quarterback and then back again as he fought off a blocker. The flanker was curling in.

The quarterback pumped once and then fired. He sent the ball on a straight line—a bullet pass—toward the flanker now racing to Lou's right.

Out of nowhere, a large hand shot up. It was Earl McGaha's as he broke through into the backfield. Earl's fingertips grazed the ball. He did not get enough of his hand on the ball to bat it down. But the deflection sent the ball floating high into the air, tumbling crazily, sure to fall several yards short of the flanker.

Lou, coming up fast, saw Marion Petosky screech to a halt in his pursuit of the flanker, reverse himself, and race back toward the falling ball. Lou veered in the same direction. He shoved falling players out of the way. He leaped over one fallen player on the ground in his path.

Marion, off balance in his desperate lunge for the ball, was stumbling. Instead of making the interception, Marion succeeded only in swatting the ball.

The ball hit Lou in the chest. Lou grabbed for it, juggled it, then held on. He tucked the ball against his stomach with both hands. His forward motion carried him crashing into the falling form of Marion. But stepping high, Lou maintained his balance. Legs churning, he kept moving forward. The hands of frantic tacklers dragged across his body, then fell away.

Suddenly Lou was outside the crowd of players. He cut upfield. In a brief instant, he thought he saw a clear path to the end zone.

The speed, power, balance, and instincts that made Lou Powers an all-state fullback in high school clicked into action. Lou had not forgotten how to run with a football. He barreled over one tackler; he sidestepped another. Max Schellenbarger materialized at Lou's side and laid low a third tackler. Lou kept going. He was crossing the Panthers' forty-yard line. Then he was hit twice simultaneously, high and low, and the tacklers dragged him to the ground on the Panthers' thirty-four-yard line.

Lou was smiling when he got to his feet. Marion Petoskey leaped at him with a giant bear hug. Max Schellenbarger was clapping both of them on the shoulder pads.

At the sideline, the Browns were cheering. They had waited a long time on this Saturday afternoon for a reason to cheer. This play was the first good break for the Browns.

Lou saw the offensive players snapping their helmet straps and heading onto the field as he ran toward the bench. Buck Foster, leaning forward, his frowning face thrust out, was saying something to Jackie. Jackie was nodding his head in sudden jerks. Then the quarterback jogged onto the field.

The Browns ganged around Lou at the sideline, laughing and cheering.

"Nice play," Otis Hildegard said a few moments later.

Lou was standing at the sideline, helmet off, watching the Browns break the huddle and line up for the attack. He was still breathing heavily from the run, but he felt like smiling. For the first time since the second half opened, he felt like linebacker Lou Powers, always in the right place at the right time to make the play.

"Thanks." Lou nodded to Hildegard. "It felt good."

On the field, Jackie took the snap from center and, without so much as a hint of a play-action fake, retreated quickly and cocked his arm for a pass, looking downfield.

Deep down the field, Spider Willard raced along the sideline. He faked a defender off-balance, zipped around him, and cut toward the center of the field. Spider was open at the five-yard line.

Jackie hurled the pass, a bit too high, too lofting—but right on target. Spider caught the ball on the three-yard line and danced into the end zone.

Lou unconsciously stepped forward at the sideline and raised his hands above his head with a cheer.

Behind him, Buck Foster was pacing a weaving path through the crowd of players. He kept saying over and over, "This game is not won yet. This game is not won yet."

14

Buck Foster was right, of course. Lou had heard the slender, frowning figure with the beak nose and the large wire-rim spectacles utter the sentence dozens of times. Buck Foster never considered a game finished until the final whistle.

Lou, standing at the sideline, watching the teams line up for the Browns' kickoff to the Panthers, told himself that anything can happen in the fourth quarter. He told himself, too, that the Lewiston Panthers were not about to give up. The Panthers had worked hard and planned carefully. They had played well. They still had a chance to get their season on the right track with a great upset victory over the Meridian Browns. The Panthers were not going to cave in.

But Lou had no doubt now that the Browns were going to win the game. The tide had turned. The touchdown gave the Browns the momentum. The two startling plays—Lou's pass interception, then Jackie's touchdown pass—changed the tone of the game completely in the span of two minutes. The Browns were ready to roll now. The expressions on the faces of all the Browns' players indicated that the horrible debacle of the first three quarters was at an end.

Johnny Douglass' kickoff, high and deep, backed the Panthers' receiver to the goal line. A charging crowd of Browns converged on the ballcarrier and nailed him at the twelve-yard line.

Lou snapped his helmet strap and led his unit onto the field to take up the defense.

In three plays—two runs and an incomplete pass—the Panthers could do no better than a net loss of two yards. They found themselves facing fourth down and twelve yards to go on their own ten-yard line. The Panthers' punting team came into the game.

The Browns were sure to gain possession of the ball in good field position—no worse than midfield, probably better. Lou glanced at his linebacking partners and smiled at them. At last they were playing football defense as the Meridian Browns were supposed to. Then the smile faded. He saw in his mind the face of the sad-eyed man. Why was the Meridian defense less than awesome earlier? Now, faced with the threat of defeat, the defense was coming alive. Why not before?

Lou tried to shake the questions out of his mind. He gathered the defensive huddle around him. On every

100

punting play, he was faced with a choice: charge in and try to block the kick, or drop back and set up a blocking wall for a good runback. Lou glanced at Foster standing at the sideline. The coach made no sign. The decision was Lou's.

"Let's block it," Lou said, and the players fanned out from the huddle to take up their positions.

Lou rocked on the balls of his feet, awaiting the snap to the punter standing in his own end zone. At the snap, Lou leaped forward, clawing his way through the tangle of bodies at the line of scrimmage. He broke through, hands raised high.

The punter took a quick step and got the kick away, barely over Lou's outstretched arms.

Donny fielded the ball on the Panthers' forty-six-yard line. He dodged away from the first tackler who made it through and scampered to the Panthers' thirty-five-yard line before he was brought down.

Lou jogged off the field, and Jackie Manteno and his offense came on. "Go get 'em," Lou said, as he passed Jackie on the field. The Browns' defense had provided a good field position. Now it was up to the offense to capitalize on it.

The quarterback nodded in response to Lou's remark. Jackie was wearing a grim expression. Gone was the cocky grin, the quick wisecrack. Jackie looked worried.

But worried or not, Jackie Manteno began unfolding one of the most spectacular displays of passing, ball handling, and faking that Lou ever had seen. A quick pass into the flat to Spider Willard picked up nine yards.

Then another, this time to Donny Campbell, gained seven yards and a first down on the nineteen-yard line. Bull Hoffman, helped by Jackie's masterful fake of a pass play, took a hand-off and barreled five yards off tackle to the Panthers' fourteen-yard line. From there, Jackie pitched out wide to Donny, and the little flanker raced thirteen yards to the one, where he was bounced out of bounds. On the next play, Bull slammed into the end zone through the center of the line.

At the Browns' bench, the players erupted into a roaring cheer. Even Buck Foster seemed to accept the fact now that the Browns were rolling and would not be stopped. He stared onto the field, frowning. But this time he did not say, "This game is not won yet."

The Panthers seemed dazed. They had played the Browns off their feet for three quarters. But now all of a sudden, mysteriously, there was no holding the Browns.

Donny and Bull were smiling when they came trotting off the field. For both of them, their spectacular play in the scoring drive wiped away horrible memories of earlier moments in the game. Donny had redeemed himself for his fumble. Bull had made up for the punchless stabs at the line in the first three quarters. Even Jackie Manteno, though not smiling, seemed less worried. The Browns were out front on the scoreboard finally.

Johnny Douglass' kick put the Browns ahead 14–7.

Again the Browns' defense held the Panthers. And again Jackie led the offense onto the field in good position, on the Panthers' thirty-eight-yard line.

And again Jackie engineered a brilliant drive. His zinging passes—Spider caught two of them, and Donny one—moved the Browns to a first down on the Panthers' seventeen-yard line. Bull Hoffman hit the center for four yards, Donny swept right end for six, and Jackie fired a pass to Spider in the corner of the end zone for the touchdown.

Johnny Douglass' kick changed the scoreboard to Panthers 7, Visitors 21.

The game ended six minutes later in a wild flurry of Lewiston passes from the shotgun formation. The desperate effort succeeded in moving the Panthers across the midfield stripe and down to the Browns' thirty-nine-yard line. But no score.

Lou, walking off the field, weary and battered, still breathing heavily from the frantic pursuit of Lewiston pass receivers, glanced at the scoreboard.

Panthers 7, Visitors 21.

Victory for the Browns by fourteen points.

The words of the sad-eyed man came back to Lou: ". . . less than three touchdowns."

Despite the noise, the atmosphere in the Browns' dressing room seemed to Lou to be more one of relief than jubilation. The players were shouting and laughing in the excitement of their come-from-behind triumph. But overlaying the elation was the fact that the Browns had had a narrow escape. They had been a whipped team at the half time. They had been a team in real danger as late as the start of the fourth quarter.

As Lou looked at the smiling faces filling the dressing room, he thought that every player—himself included—deserved mixed feelings. All of them with a reason to rejoice also had a reason to regret. The same players who won the game in the fourth quarter had contributed to the disaster of the first three quarters.

The laughter in the dressing room had a strained and forced air about it.

Lou peeled off his jersey slowly. Even in the steamy dressing room, the air hitting his skin felt cool. When he turned to walk to the showers, Lou spotted Buck Foster in whispered conversation near the door with Scotty Hanks.

The scene puzzled Lou. He could not recall ever seeing the Browns' publicity man in the dressing room after a game. Scotty Hanks' job was in the press box, high above the seats in the stadium. His task was to feed statistics and other information to the sportswriters hammering out their stories. The needs of the sportswriters always kept Scotty in the press box long after the last of the Browns' players had finished showering and dressing.

Scotty was nodding as Foster spoke.

When Lou returned from the showers, Scotty Hanks was gone and Foster, frown in place, was standing in the center of the room with the game ball in his hand. There was no question about who was going to receive the game ball. Foster walked straight to Jackie Manteno and handed the ball to the quarterback.

15

The face on the front page of the newspaper jumped out at Lou. He was standing at a newsstand in the sprawling terminal of the Philadelphia airport. Donny Campbell was at his side. Earl McGaha was standing behind Lou. Other players were milling around in the area, awaiting their boarding call

The end of the Lewiston game was more than three hours behind them. For all the Browns, the relaxation from the strain, the contact, the tension of the game was complete now.

The long bus ride through the Pennsylvania countryside and then through the city suburbs to the airport was, as usual, a quiet time for the players. The unwinding process was under way. Then a catered dinner of steak, potatoes, and salad, served in a holding room set up specially for the team, left everyone restored. They were tired, but happy with victory, and comfortable, when they walked from dinner toward their chartered plane.

The players stopped off at the newsstand. The early editions of the Sunday morning papers were there. The newspapers trumpeted the word on page one that the Meridian Browns had marked up another victory. The players bought the papers. They wanted to read about themselves.

Lou bent over to pick one off the stack. He glanced casually at the front page. Then he felt his heartbeat quicken. His face suddenly flushed with warmth.

The sad-eyed little man, his fixed smile no longer there, was one of three men in a photograph on the front page. He was the man on the right. The headline beneath the photograph said: *Three Arrested in Scheme to Fix College Football.*

Lou blinked at the picture. The man was not wearing the beige trenchcoat. The thought was totally irrelevant. Lou read the caption under the picture. Two of the names meant nothing to him; two of the faces meant nothing to him. He never had heard the names; he never had seen the faces. Nor did the name of the man on the right mean anything without the sad-eyed face that went with it. Lou's eyes lingered over the name in the caption: Charles Dryden.

So that was his name—Charles Dryden.

"You want to take the paper with you, bub, or are you just going to read it here?"

Lou looked up, startled.

The man behind the counter was wearing a sweatshirt and thick glasses with heavy rims that had slid down on his nose. He was taking coins from other customers while he spoke to Lou. He did so without looking at them. His eyes were on Lou.

"Yeah, Powers," said Donny Campbell with a smile. "This isn't a lending library, you know."

"Right," the man behind the counter said. His expression did not change.

"Sorry," Lou said. He dug into a trouser pocket and handed over a pair of quarters for the Sunday paper.

The man took the coins and turned to other customers.

Donny picked up a paper behind Lou, and they walked together toward the boarding ramp. Lou, with some effort, kept the newspaper under his arm casually as they walked.

A student manager stood at the gate with an airline official checking off the names of the players as they entered the boarding area.

A few minutes later they were on the plane. Lou and Donny slid into seats together.

Unconsciously Lou sat up straight and turned, looking around the half-filled plane. He was searching for the face of Jackie Manteno. Jackie had not boarded the plane yet.

"Look at this—a college football gambling scandal," Donny said.

"That's what I was looking at back at the newsstand."

Donny glanced at the story quickly and then, with an impish smile, said, "Why doesn't anybody ever offer me a payoff? I need the money."

"Looks like it's too late for these guys to help you," Lou said.

Donny dropped the front section of the paper on the floor under the seat and shifted his concentration to the game story in the sports section.

Lou scanned the gambling story quickly, first the opening paragraphs on the front page, then the additional material on an inside page. He was looking for any mention of Meridian University. There was only one, a statement from Buck Foster deploring efforts to corrupt football players. Lou nodded slightly to himself. That explained Scotty Hanks' presence in the dressing room. He was telling Buck Foster of the development and getting a comment from the coach for the writers in the press box. Clearly, part of Scotty's report to Foster had been the good news that there was no indication of Meridian University involvement.

Lou returned to the beginning of the story on the front page and read carefully through to the end.

The facts were simple: The three men had approached players at four schools in the Midwest. The men offered payments up to $1500 a game for controlling the point spread. The players had reported the overtures to their coaches. The coaches had notified school officials. The school officials had called in the FBI. The FBI had arrested the three, all known gamblers in the Chicago area.

Lou frowned. His left hand was trembling.
The story quoted the U.S. district attorney:

At the moment, we have no knowledge of any
other players at any other schools being approached.
There is, of course, a possibility that others were
approached and have not come forward. As far as
we know, no players have accepted bribes. There
are no charges pending involving any players.

Lou glanced at Donny. Donny was engrossed in the
game story in the sports section.

"There you are, Powers," he said. He pointed to a
photograph. "There you are, running with the interception."

Lou leaned over. He had not seen a picture of himself
running with the football since he played fullback in
high school. "Yep," he said, "there I am." He leaned
back in his seat. He stared out the window at the black-
ness.

The plane passed over a twinkling cluster of lights—a
small town down there—and then passed over another.

His chin on his fist, watching the night go by outside
the plane's window, Lou wondered what the arrests
meant for him. Maybe the end of the mess—really the
end.

The sad-eyed man and his partners were under arrest.
They were headed for jail for sure. Their game was
ended. With four players ready to testify, conviction was
certain.

Lou flinched slightly at the thought of the four players reporting the gamblers' overtures to their coaches. The players had, each of them, gone through the same ordeal that Lou had suffered. First the surprise, the puzzlement. Then the indignation. They were insulted that a gambler might think they were for sale. Then, for sure, they had had those brief moments when they knew they could buy the deal and—probably—get away with it, with no one the wiser. The thought frightened them. Suspicion followed. Were teammates on the take? Confusion about what to do, how to escape the web, settled in. Finally the easy rationalization: reject the deal, say nothing, let it blow over. Avoid the cloud of suspicion.

But in the end the four players at the other schools had decided that they had to report the incident. Lou Powers had decided that he did not.

Lou never had heard the names of any of the players involved. Only one of them played for a team on the Browns' schedule—Miller State, the eighth team on the list.

Lou found a sense of comfort in the fact that the players were unknown to him. They were not Lou Powers. They were not everybody's all-American. They were not candidates for the Heisman Trophy. They were not being mentioned as the number-one choice in the pro draft. Their faces were not on the cover of *Sports Illustrated* magazine. They did not have the same stake involved as Lou Powers did. They did not have so much to lose. For them, it was easy. For Lou Powers, it was not.

Jackie Manteno walked past Lou's seat, heading for the washroom. Lou watched the quarterback's back as he made his way along the aisle. The plane was darkened now, except for a half-dozen reading lamps sending needles of light down from the ceiling. Lou could not see Jackie's face when he opened the washroom door and stepped inside.

If Jackie—or anyone on the Browns' team—was involved, could the mess really be over for Lou Powers? Could Meridian possibly escape untouched? Could Lou Powers escape? Would Jackie, or anyone else, come forward now? No.

If Lou Powers, innocent of any wrongdoing, was going to keep his secret, so would anyone guilty of taking a payoff. Lou blinked. He ran the thought back through his mind: If Lou Powers was going to keep his secret. . . .

Without deciding, Lou had in fact decided. He was not going to go to Buck Foster with his story of a gambler's overture. Not now. It was impossible now. There was no answer for Lou to Buck Foster's first terrible question: Why did you not report the incident immediately? There was no answer for Lou at all.

16

"Did you hear about Jackie?"

Donny Campbell was standing next to the table in the Brown House restaurant where Lou and Paige were having dinner. The popular eating establishment was packed with the usual Sunday-evening crowd of students. Lou and Paige were seated at a small table near the rear of the room.

Lou looked up. "No," he said. "What's happened?"

Lou knew what was coming. He saw bad news written in Donny's serious expression. The slender little flanker wore his feelings on his face. He grinned and laughed when he scored a touchdown. He cried when he fumbled. Now he was frowning. His lips, in a straight line, were pressed tightly together. It was bad news. Usually

112

bad news about a teammate fell into one of two categories—a sinking grade-point average that jeopardized football eligibility or an accidental injury. But this time Low saw in his mind only the face of the sad-eyed man named Charles Dryden.

Donny glanced around at the neighboring tables. Nobody was paying attention to his conversation with Lou. He lowered his voice. "He's in the gambling scandal."

Lou stared at Donny without speaking.

"It just came out," Donny said. "It's on the radio. I heard it driving over here. Just a few minutes ago."

"Sit down," Lou said.

Donny turned and borrowed a chair from a table with only three diners. He squeezed himself into the aisle next to Lou's small table for two.

"But Jackie!" Paige said suddenly.

She was genuinely surprised. Lou and Paige had discussed the gambling scandal during their long afternoon walk through the campus. Lou had been strongly tempted to tell her about his encounter with the man. After all, the episode seemed over with the arrests of the gamblers. But he never was able to find exactly the right moment, and he had let the discussion pass without telling her. Now he was glad. The episode was not over. On the contrary. The net was beginning to widen. The net had extended to Meridian University. It might reach far enough to snare Lou Powers. But maybe not, if he kept quiet. There was no need to tell Paige. No need to worry her—not yet.

"What did they say? On the radio?"

"One of the gamblers blew the whistle on Jackie. The one named Dryden, or something like that. He's turning state's evidence or something, trying to get a lighter sentence for himself, you know. He told 'em Jackie was on the take."

Lou felt a shiver. If Charles Dryden was telling all he knew in an effort to negotiate a light sentence, could the name of Lou Powers be far behind?

"Jeez," Lou said.

"Yeah. And to think, he won the game ball as the most valuable player of the game."

"For his play in the second half," Lou said absently. He remembered Jackie's off-center passing of the first half. And he remembered the scoreboard at the finish —21–7—less than three touchdowns.

"Were any other players named?" Lou asked.

"No, just Jackie."

"I mean, any other players from any other schools."

"No, just Jackie." Donny paused. "But you can bet they're looking."

"What do you mean?"

"Well, players at four schools reported being approached. That blew the thing open. That looked like the whole show. But now they know that at least one player at one other school was approached and bought the deal. There must be others."

Lou glanced at Paige. She was staring at him intently. He shifted his gaze quickly back to Donny. "Yeah, I guess so."

They were silent a moment. Lou sensed the unasked question between them: Was Jackie the only one? Were others of the Browns' players involved? Who? Lou did not ask the question. Neither did Donny.

Lou broke the silence. "What did they say that Jackie did? I mean, do they know exactly. . . ."

Donny leaned forward, and his voice dropped almost to a whisper. "The Danton game, and the Lewiston game too—held the score down below the point spread." Donny paused. "For fifteen hundred dollars a game," he said.

Lou nodded. He knew the price.

"It's hard to believe," Donny said. He sounded as if he were talking to himself. "It's incredible. Jackie had everything going for him. He was almost a sure all-American—as a freshman! He'd have been a Heisman Trophy candidate by his senior year, for sure. He could have been a star in the pro ranks."

"Yeah," Lou said.

Lou felt Paige's eyes on him. This time he avoided her glance.

"Foster, I guess he knows."

"I think he must have found out this morning," Donny said. "You remember, he called Jackie back when we were leaving the screening room."

Lou's mind went back to the early-morning screening of the game film in the basement of the field house. Lou had been there, as always. So was Jackie. So was Brad Chapman. So were a half-dozen other players. Donny was one of them. The turnout was an unusually large

115

one—a tribute, Lou believed, to the Browns' serious concern about a poorly played game.

The screening of the game film had been an embarrassment for all of them. The first three quarters were horrible. Dave Emerson missed blocks. Donny Campball fumbled. Lou, straining to extend himself, got caught out of position time and again. Spider Willard dropped a surefire pass. Jackie fumbled once on a handoff, threw an interception, and missed the mark on a half-dozen of his throws.

Through it all, as the figures danced on the screen, Buck Foster and his assistant coaches said little. The screening itself was punishment enough for the somber group of players gathered in the darkened room. They did not need lashing words from the coaches. The errors in the first three quarters were so obvious that they needed no comment.

When the film finally ended and the lights came on, Scotty Hanks was standing in the back of the room. He was not smiling. He barely responded to the greetings of the players filing out of the room. He moved over to Foster. They spoke in whispers for a moment.

Then Foster stepped into the corridor and called out to the players heading for the stairway, "Manteno, I need to see you for a minute."

Jackie had turned and walked back while Lou and the others continued up the stairway and out of the field house.

"Yeah," Lou said. "That must have been it. The reporters, or somebody, called Scotty at home, and he came to the field house to tell Foster. That must've been it."

"Well, we've got Brad," Donny said.

Lou wondered if Brad Chapman knew yet that he was back in the starting quarterback role with the Meridian Browns. Brad's dedication was going to pay off, for himself and for the Browns. Brad's determination to stick it out, practicing hard, attending the Sunday-morning screenings, would now put him in a strong position, fully prepared to step into the job. A lesser person, hurt and embarrassed, might have slacked off in his efforts or quit the team entirely. Brad's readiness was a bonus for the Browns, and it would go a long way toward offsetting the loss of Jackie Manteno.

"What do you think we ought to do?" Donny asked.

"Do?" Lou repeated. He paused. "The first thing I think we ought to do is get out of here right now. Everybody in the place is going to know about Jackie in a few minutes. I'd rather not be here when they find out."

The campus was quiet in the chilly autumn evening as Lou and Paige walked toward her dormitory.

Paige broke the silence as they walked. "You weren't surprised, were you?"

"What?"

"About Jackie. You weren't surprised, were you?"

Lou took a deep breath. "I suspected that something might be going on."

"You suspected because the gamblers made you an offer, too, didn't they?"

17

By the hour of practice on Monday afternoon, Lou
Powers knew what he had to do. Events were rolling
over him. He could see now what he should have done
in the first place. He should have gone to Buck Foster.
He should have told his story, turned over the money,
and taken the heat. He should have done it immediately.
Reporting the incident would have been tough, unpleasant, perhaps even dangerous, but necessary.

Each development—and they were coming fast—made
it more difficult for Lou to come forward and tell his
story. But at the same time, each development made it
more necessary than before for him to disclose his involvement.

Lou could see the situation clearly now.

The first encounter. Why didn't you report it, Powers?

The arrests. Why did you wait until the gamblers were knocked out of business, Powers? Then the shocking revelation that Jackie Manteno was shaving points. Why did you wait until a teammate had been caught, Powers? What next? Whatever, it could only make matters worse. Are you speaking up now because you were afraid they were getting close to you, Powers?

Paige had stated the case with unassailable logic. They were sitting on the front steps of Paige's dormitory. They had walked across the campus, talking, from the Brown House with Donny's horrible news still ringing in their ears. Paige's correct conclusion that Lou had been approached had confused and surprised Lou at first. But then he was relieved to be able to unburden himself. The porch light cast funny shadows in the nippy night air. They sat and talked for an hour.

"It's bound to come out, sooner or later, you know." Paige said. "It's better that you be the one to tell it."

Lou could not think of a rebuttal.

The next morning, all across the campus, the unasked question between Lou and Donny was being asked by everyone: Was Jackie the only one?

Lou first heard the question at the breakfast table at the Sigma Chi house. He heard it in a corridor changing classes. He heard it at lunch in the Student Union cafeteria. He read it in the newspapers. The question was everywhere.

The entire team had fallen under the shadow of suspicion, and the shadow was sure to widen when Lou Powers stepped forward with his story. It was one thing for a freshman quarterback, young and unsophisticated, bedazzled by the glittering world of big-time college football, to make a mistake. It was quite another for Lou Powers, a senior, the defensive captain, an all-American, the best in a long line of great Meridian linebackers, to hide his involvement in the scandal, innocent or not. And there would be the question: Was Lou Powers telling the truth?

Lou wiped the question from his mind and walked from his final class of the day to the field house.

The time was half past two. The players would be gathering for practice at three o'clock. Buck Foster always was there early, putting the finishing touches on the practice schedule with his assistant coaches.

Lou pulled open the front door and stepped into the lobby of the field house.

"You're early for practice." Kathleen Norris, the ticket manager, athletic department secretary, and— some said—the assistant athletic director, was smiling at Lou from her office off the lobby. She was a woman in her fifties, tiny, gray-haired, who had spent half her life working in the athletic department at Meridian University. She had seen the great ones come and go.

"I need to see Coach Foster for a minute." He didn't want to appear worried and tried to smile. "It's something that I need to talk to him about before practice."

"I'm sorry, Lou, but Coach Foster isn't here. He hasn't been here all day. He's over at the Administration building. He's in meetings with the president and the chairman of the board of trustees." She paused. "The Jackie Manteno trouble, you know."

"Oh."

"Coach Hildegard is downstairs," she said.

"No, I—no thanks, Mrs. Norris. I'll catch Coach Foster after practice. It'll wait."

In groups of twos and threes, the players trooped from the dressing room to the screening room, their cleated shoes clacking on the concrete floor. They dropped into seats and waited. There was none of the usual wisecracking.

The Browns didn't act like an undefeated team that was riding at the top of the national polls, headed for a national championship. They were subdued and uneasy, a team coming off a poor performance only to be shaken by the devastating news that their quarterback was shaving points.

At the front of the room, Buck Foster was huddled with his assistant coaches, awaiting the arrival of the last of the players from the dressing room. Otis Hildegard and Bernie Carlisle were there, ready to critique the Lewiston game with excerpts from the game film. George Coleman, the Browns' veteran scout, was there to tell the team about the Athens Tigers, next team up on the Browns' schedule.

Lou spotted Brad Chapman and walked over and sat down next to him. "You okay?"

Brad smiled slightly. "Yeah, I'm okay." The senior

121

quarterback, one of the nation's best, had won back his spot in the starting lineup in the worst possible way.

Lou watched Buck Foster. He wondered what the coach was going to tell the team. He wondered too if the coach knew more than the rest of the world. Was anyone else on the team involved? Lou glanced around the room. Nobody but Jackie seemed to be missing. A good sign.

The replacement of Jackie Manteno with Brad Chapman was no great problem for the Meridian Browns. Sure, they were a stronger team with Manteno at quarterback than with Chapman, but Brad was close to being Jackie's match. In fact, the choice of Manteno over Chapman at the end of the preseason drills could have been made on the flip of a coin.

However, Lou knew that the problems of the Meridian Browns now were bigger than the simple changing of faces at the quarterback position. There were other worries swirling around the team.

Not the least of them, Lou knew, was suspicion. He could feel the ugly symptoms growing in his own mind. He watched Spider Willard and Bull Hoffman walk into the room together and take seats. Spider had juggled and dropped too many passes in the Lewiston game. Bull Hoffman botched a big play in the Danton game and turned in a subpar performance for three quarters against Lewiston.

Donny Campbell followed them into the room. It was inconceivable to Lou that Donny Campbell was involved. He and Lou had been close friends for four years. Donny

122

had carried the word about Jackie to Lou. He had been concerned, troubled, confused. But his fumble had set up the Lewiston touchdown. With a frown, Lou reflected that Donny, who never had owned a car, had one now. It was not a new car. But no car was cheap these days. The money had to come from somewhere.

Another troubling thought occurred to Lou as he watched Donny take a seat. Donny would find it inconceivable that he was involved and failed to report the incident. So was it impossible that Donny might be involved?

Foster stepped to the edge of the low platform at the front of the room. "Anybody else in the locker room, Campbell?"

"No, sir."

"Let's get started."

Hands in pockets, feet planted far apart, Foster scowled out over the crowd in front of him—large young men, made larger by hulking shoulder pads and hip pads.

Was he looking for someone in particular? Lou felt that Foster's gaze rested longer on him than the others.

"I won't mince words," he said. "Jackie Manteno is gone—off the team, out of school. He may face criminal charges. All of us know why. The story doesn't need retelling here." Foster spoke in clipped, staccato tones. He looked around his audience again. There was no sound in the room. "I trust that he was the only one involved. The gambler, Dryden, named Jackie. You should know that he has named no other members of our team. None. And I've not heard from any other source

—that is, from any of you—that any other of our players were involved."

Lou watched and listened, unblinking. He hoped that Foster's eyes would not meet his at this moment.

"So we are closing the book on it," Foster said. "It was an unfortunate, even tragic, incident for one very unwise young man and for this team. But now—today— we put it behind us. We close the book on it. We've got a game coming up on Saturday, a tough game. We've got a lot of work to do."

Lou wished more than ever that he had been able to see Foster before practice. The coach's statement amounted to still another development that made it more difficult than before for him to come forward. But he knew that he must do so.

Foster stood there another moment, unmoving, frowning out at the faces in front of him. Then he stepped back and nodded at Otis Hildegard and Bernie Carlisle to begin their critiques of the Lewiston game.

The practice on this Monday was hard. Normally, the plan for Monday called for light play drills and little else. Usually it was a time for the final nursing of bruises and scrapes from last Saturday's game. It was the beginning of the build-up for next Saturday's game, a slow beginning, designed to have the team at peak efficiency at week's end. But today the coaches were determined to snap the players' thoughts back from Jackie Manteno to the game of football. They ran the team hard from start to finish.

At the end, Lou ran the full distance down the sloping field to the field house. He wanted to be the first to shower, dress, and get out of the locker room. Now, after all these days of turmoil, Lou could not wait to tell Buck Foster that he had been approached by the gambler.

Looking back, Lou was grateful that he still had the opportunity to take the story to Foster himself. He was lucky. Charles Dryden had named Jackie Manteno. He might have named Lou Powers too. Then where would Lou be?

The thought frightened him. He had come so close, he knew now, to losing everything. Ever since the gamblers' arrest, the clock had been ticking toward the moment when the full story somehow got out.

Lou understood how dumb he had been now. He saw clearly the dangers he had been courting—dangers to his record, his reputation, his future.

Hurrying toward the locker room, Lou suddenly had a scary thought. The clock was *still* ticking. His heartbeat quickened. At this very moment, Charles Dryden might be telling the FBI agents in Chicago that he had given money to Lou Powers. There might be someone, somewhere, telling the FBI agents that he had seen Lou Powers with Charles Dryden at the Blue Moon truck stop. Possibly Jackie Manteno, through Charles Dryden, knew of Lou's involvement. Jackie might, for whatever reasons, tell about it.

Lou stepped up the speed of his run to the locker room. He felt a terrible urgency. Why hadn't he intercepted Foster before practice and spilled out the story?

He could have done so. Why had he decided to wait until after practice? He might have lost his last chance. He might have lost it by five minutes—or one minute.

For a moment Lou considered going straight to Foster's office, sweaty and dirty and still wearing his shoulder pads. No, he told himself. He was getting panicky. He entered the locker room. If only his luck would hold for a few more minutes. . . . It was going to be a great relief.

18

"Powers!"

Lou was stuffing in his shirt and buckling his trousers in front of his locker in the dressing room. Around him, other players were toweling off.

Lou was ahead of them. He had peeled off his practice uniform and hurried into the shower. This was not the day to allow himself the luxury of sitting, still breathing heavily, for a few minutes on the bench in front of his locker. He was in a hurry. In the shower he had doused himself with water—first the hot, with a quick soaping, then the cold—and stepped out immediately. This was not the day to savor those few extra minutes in the shower, to enjoy the hot needles of water washing away the sweat and the soreness and the weariness. He was in a hurry.

The clock was still ticking somewhere. It was ticking

off the seconds he had left to get to Foster first with the story of his involvement in the gambling scandal. The ticking in Lou's mind seemed to get faster and faster.

He turned at the sound of his name.

"Coach's office—right now." The student manager spoke the words from the dressing room doorway. Then he disappeared back into the corridor, toward the equipment room.

"Right," Lou called out.

Lou frowned. A summons to Buck Foster's office was a rare event for a Meridian Browns player. Foster always did his talking to his players on the practice field or in the screening room. He had little use for individual visits with his players, even the defensive captain of the Browns. On any other day, the command would have puzzled Lou, nothing more. But this day was different. His frown deepened.

Several players cast questioning glances in Lou's direction. Lou responded with raised eyebrows and a shrug.

Lou picked his jacket off the hook in the locker and closed the locker door. He slipped the lock in place, clicked it shut, and walked out of the dressing room.

He tried to remember the last time Buck Foster had summoned him to the office, but could not. There had not been a previous summons.

"Calm down," Lou told himself. "Take it easy."

The door to Foster's office was closed. Lou knocked.

"Come in," said Foster.

Lou opened the door and stepped inside.

"Close the door, Lou." Foster's voice was quiet.

Scotty Hanks was standing with him.

Lou looked from one to the other. They were a somber pair. Both wore serious expressions. For Foster, the frown was normal. But the effervescent publicity man of the Meridian Browns had seemed never to frown. Not until yesterday, when he was waiting for Foster after the early-morning screening of the game film to deliver the bad news about Jackie Manteno. Scotty had been frowning then. And he was frowning now.

Lou's uneasiness deepened. In his mind, the clock had stopped ticking. The time had run out.

"Sit down, Lou," Foster said.

Lou took a seat on the heavy leather sofa alongside the wall opposite Foster's desk.

Foster perched himself, arms folded, on the corner of the heavy table he used for a desk. He was watching Lou. "Okay, Scotty," Foster said, without taking his eyes off Lou.

Scotty crossed over in front of the coach and sat on an overstuffed chair at an angle to Lou. He leaned forward, elbows on knees, hands clasped loosely together.

Lou shifted uncomfortably on the sofa. This meeting, called by Foster, was not shaping up as a happy one.

"Lou, we've got something serious on our hands." Scotty spoke softly, calmly. "The television network people from Chicago—the people who were here at practice last week, you remember—have come up with a film segment showing you speaking at the end of the practice with a man they say is Charles Dryden."

Lou felt all the air go out of his lungs. He sucked

the air back in. He started to try to say something. The words would not come out.

"They were editing the film for clips of Jackie Manteno to use on tonight's news, and there you were," Scotty said. "Somebody recognized Dryden talking to you—or at least they claim the man was Dryden."

"I—"

Scotty lifted a hand, and Lou waited. "There's more. They used the film on tonight's news just a few minutes ago. I tried to get them to hold off until we had a chance to talk with you. After all, Dryden could have spoken with anybody. That doesn't necessarily mean anything. A lot of people start up conversations with our players coming off the practice field. But they weren't about to hold off using the film clip. They had something hot, and they had it exclusively. So they went ahead with it on tonight's news, and the whole world has been told by that network that Lou Powers was talking with a central figure in the gambling scandal." Scotty leaned back, finished.

Lou glanced at Foster. The coach was waiting. "Yes," Lou said finally. He caught himself clenching and unclenching his right fist, and he stopped.

"Yes, what?" Foster snapped.

Lou swallowed and cleared his throat. He said, "Yes, it's true. It was Dryden I was talking to."

Foster kept his eyes on Lou. He did not speak.

Lou recalled Paige's statement: "It's bound to come out sooner or later, you know. It's better that you be the one to tell it."

130

Scotty leaned forward again. "You'd better tell us about it," he said. "All about it—everything."

Lou glanced at Scotty. Then he turned to Foster. He began at the beginning and told about the casual encounter with a sad-eyed man wearing a beige trenchcoat, walking across the campus. He told about the envelope thrust into his hand in the corridor outside the dressing room after the Danton game. He told about opening the envelope in his room and counting the money. He left nothing out of the telling.

He described his feelings—his puzzlement at being selected as a target by the gambler, his fears about the gambler's contact becoming public knowledge, his horror at the thought of how easily he could do the job for the man, his confusion about whether to tell Buck Foster about the gambler's approach.

Lou paused before mentioning his suspicions. He took a breath and plunged ahead. He told of worrying about who else on the team might be involved. He named no names. Then he told of his suspicions of Jackie and his doubts about the flimsy evidence against the quarterback —one pass interception, nothing else.

He described his feelings of guilt. He told of his nervousness and then his anger at the Blue Moon truck stop.

He told of his sense of release when he decided, just last night, to tell the story to Foster, and finally he described his feelings at this moment. "I feel as if I've been kicked in the chest—and that I deserved it," he said.

Foster stood up. He walked across his office, away

131

from his desk and Lou. He turned and walked back. "What do you think, Scotty?"

Scotty did not hesitate. "I think that Lou ought to tell the story, exactly that way, to the authorities and to the television and newspaper people."

"A press conference?" Foster asked.

"Yes."

Foster frowned at Scotty a moment without answering. One of the coach's unbending rules prohibited his players from giving direct interviews to the news media. If reporters had questions for a player, they went through Scotty. He got the quotes the reporters wanted and relayed them. Foster allowed nothing else. He had been criticized, mainly by the press, for the rule. He was treating his players like children. Couldn't they speak for themselves? He was censoring his players' remarks. What was he hiding? But Foster stuck by his rule. He had seen too many good teams wrecked by talking players. He was going to have no prima donna players building themselves up in the press, no disgruntled second stringers doing their moaning in public, no overly enthusiastic players predicting a big victory the next Saturday. Foster was convinced there was nothing to gain and much to lose from players speaking for publication.

"No," Foster said finally. "No press conference."

"This is different," Scotty said.

"No."

Scotty shrugged. "Whatever you say."

Lou found himself with mixed feelings while the two

discussed how best Lou Powers might try to salvage his reputation. The thought of a press conference—television lights, reporters from all the newspapers and magazines —was a bit frightening. But Lou knew he could do it, and the idea of getting his side of the story before the public in the most forceful way appealed to him. But what he thought did not matter. Foster had said no.

"Prepare a statement, Scotty," Foster said. "You heard Lou's story. You can write the statement. Issue it right away. Otherwise, we will confine our talking to the U.S. district attorney's people, and you can say that in the statement. Okay?"

"Okay."

Scotty was gone.

Buck Foster was perched on the corner of the table again. "I won't lecture you," Foster said. "Suffice it to say you acted stupidly. You should have known better."

"I know that now."

"You were confused, frightened. I understand."

Lou nodded, waiting. Foster said nothing. Finally Lou asked, "Am I . . . ?"

"Are you what?"

"Am I still on the team?"

"As it stands now, yes."

19

In other words, Buck Foster believed Lou Powers' story —for the moment, at least. But Lou wondered who else would believe it.

When he arrived at the Sigma Chi house for his usual late dinner following practice, he drew blank stares and embarrassed silence from the few students he encountered. He made his way alone to the kitchen.

The word was spreading. They all knew. By now those who had not seen the newscast were hearing the story from others. The startling news showed in their faces and in their silence.

Lou wanted to blurt out, "Wait until you've heard my side of it." But he said nothing.

He understood their shock. For four years Lou Powers had been an ornament of his fraternity. He was a celebrity among friends. They shared in his fame and glory. Now they shared in his shame and embarrassment.

Lou understood, too, their discomfort when his eyes met theirs. The evidence of Lou's conversation with Charles Dryden had been there on the television screen for all to see. Perhaps there was nothing wrong in the conversation. But to ask was to say that Lou owed an explanation. So they said nothing. And neither did Lou.

Lou got his plate out of the kitchen and walked into the empty dining room and sat down at a table. He looked at his wristwatch. The time was seven o'clock. The other players, taking their late dinners, were hearing the news for the first time in the fraternity houses, the dormitories, and the rooming houses around the campus.

Lou ate his dinner hurriedly. Then he stepped into the telephone booth in the foyer. He had two calls to make. One would be quick. The other would take a while. He decided to make the short one first.

"Paige, you've heard?"

"Yes, I saw it on television. They called me out of my room when it came on. It's horrible." She paused. "Are you all right?"

"Well, Foster believed me."

"Thank God for that. It looked bad on television."

"I'm sure it did."

Next Lou placed a long-distance call. His father in Oklahoma answered the telephone.

"You've heard the news?"

"Yes."

"Did you see it on television?"

"Yes, we saw it. What is it all about?"

Once more Lou told his story, from the beginning, leaving nothing out. Then he walked out the front door of the Sigma Chi house. He did not want to be there when the telephone started ringing.

The next morning was no better. There was the photograph—Lou Powers in profile, Charles Dryden facing the camera—on page one of the morning newspaper. They were in conversation. The clip from the television film left no doubt. Lou Powers and the gambler were talking to each other.

The other students at the long table in the dining room waited in silence while Lou looked at the newspaper.

The headline read: *TV Film Links Lou Powers to 'Fix' Scandal Figure.* And beneath the main headline, the subheading in smaller type read: *Star Linebacker Admits Contact, Denies Shaving Points for Payoff.*

The story contained Lou's account of what happened, to be sure. But the main thrust was the sensational discovery, on film, that the Meridian Browns' linebacker had talked with Charles Dryden about shaving points and had not reported the incident to the authorities.

Lou read Buck Foster's statement to the press: "Lou Powers is an innocent victim. He is an outstanding young man, as well as an outstanding football player. He is guilty of poor judgment in not reporting the contact to me immediately. But he is guilty of nothing else."

Clearly, Buck Foster was standing behind him. Lou felt a strange mix of emotions—warm appreciation for

136

the coach's support and guilt for what he considered his betrayal in not going to the coach in the first place.

Lou laid down the paper and began eating his breakfast.

"It'll blow over," one student said.

Another leaned across to Lou. "I don't see why you didn't just go to Foster in the first place."

Everyone within earshot looked up, awaiting the answer.

"Right now, neither do I," Lou said.

On the campus, Lou caught people staring at him as he headed for his first class of the day. Everyone was buzzing over the second shock wave in two days to hit the Meridian Browns' football team. First Jackie Manteno, caught and expelled. Now Lou Powers, implicated somehow. Who else? Who will be next?

And, too: What really was the extent of Lou Powers' implication? Conversations on the campus seemed to stop when Lou walked past a group.

And in his modern European history class the professor, with a knowing smile, looked out over the students taking their seats and said, "I am pleased to see you here this morning, Mr. Powers."

A chuckle rippled through the classroom.

Lou looked up, startled out of his thoughts, with a frown on his face.

Professor Edgar Schafer, a birdlike little man with unruly rust-colored hair, stood there, smiling, awaiting Lou's response. Lou had seen Professor Schafer in action before. Whether the mistake was made by a tardy stu-

dent, an unprepared student—or even a historical figure
—Professor Schafer never let vulnerability go by without
a barb.

"Thank you, sir," Lou said with a straight face. "I am
pleased to be here."

The wave of small chuckles rolled back across the
classroom.

Lou busied himself arranging his notebook for the
upcoming lecture.

The afternoon was worse.

"Coach wants you, Lou," the student manager said.
"Right now."

Lou was heading into a classroom. "Okay," he said.
He turned and walked out of the building, buttoning his
jacket to the neck against the light drizzle that had
started falling.

He passed two students from the other direction. He
did not know them. But out of habit, he nodded to them.
As they passed, he heard the words, "But he admits he
took the money in the first place." Lou did not look back
at them.

His worst fears were coming true. He recalled the chill
he felt when he first opened the gambler's envelope and
counted the money. The same shivering fear returned
now. Guilty or not, he was tainted with suspicion. He
knew what was coming when he first saw the money. No
matter that he returned the money, that he rejected the
deal, that he never tried to fix a point spread. No matter

that he was innocent. The taint of suspicion was there. Lou saw the question hovering over him for the rest of his life.

When the time came for the Heisman Trophy voting, and the nation's best collegiate linebacker was one of the candidates, there was the question: Did Lou Powers buy the gambler's deal? When the pro teams gathered in the spring for the annual draft, and the nation's best linebacker was expected to be the first selection, there was the question again: Did Lou Powers buy the gambler's deal? And when the law schools considered his application, and the grades were satisfactory, there was the question: Did Lou Powers buy the gambler's deal?

Perhaps worst of all there was Lou Powers' place in the legend of Meridian University football. Lou had entered Meridian to become a part of the legend. He had worked, sweated, and taken injuries to assure his place. His record spoke for itself, but now he was in danger of being remembered for something else. "Say, wasn't Lou Powers the one in the gambling scandal? You know, the one with Jackie Manteno?" And: "Well, after all, he took the money, didn't he? And he never said anything about it until he got caught. Yeah, I know he said he gave it back, but. . . ."

Lou ducked into the chemistry building to escape the drizzling rain for half a block and came out the other side. He jogged the final few yards across the brick courtyard to the front door of the field house.

He walked through the lobby quickly, without looking

139

in the direction of Kathleen Norris' office. Downstairs, he found the door to Foster's office closed, and he knocked.

The door opened, and Foster said, "Come in, Lou."

Lou stepped inside the office and nodded to Scotty Hanks.

Foster closed the office door.

Two men in business suits got to their feet from the sofa. They were young men, not more than a few years older than Lou. They both wore friendly smiles.

"These gentlemen are from the FBI," Foster said.

20

"You realize, of course, that you are, by your own admission, guilty of being an accessory to a conspiracy." The young man speaking was the shorter and stockier of the two FBI agents. He spoke in a soft, matter-of-fact voice, his face expressionless.

The words hit Lou like an electric shock. Of course, it was so. The minute the payoff was offered, Lou knew that a crime had been committed. He had not reported it. Lou knew the legal term: accessory after the fact. It simply had never occurred to him. Through all the tortuous hours of trying to find a way out of his involvement, Lou never had recognized, as he should have, his obligation to report the committing of a crime. He was innocent of shaving points for a payoff. That was all he had thought about—his innocence of shaving points and the need to maintain the *appearance* of innocence. Just that. Nothing else.

"But I. . . ." Lou looked at Foster. The coach was frowning at Lou. Foster's face showed nothing else.

Lou let the half-started sentence hang in the air unfinished. His mind was whirling. Was he, innocent as he was, going to jail on a technicality? Or *was* it a technicality? Of course not. It was a crime, withholding knowledge of a crime. A criminal charge meant—what? Yes, a trial. Conviction meant—what? Probation at the best, jail at the worst. It didn't matter. Either way it was the end of the world for Lou Powers. Lou had struggled with himself these ten days to keep his world from crashing down, and now he knew it was too late. His world *had* crashed. Without his realizing, it had crashed the first day he kept the money and said nothing. While he had been standing in his room in the Sigma Chi house counting the money, his world was tumbling down around him. While he had been telling Paige at the party that nothing was wrong, everything was going wrong. So long ago. So long ago. And he had not known it for ten days.

Suddenly Lou stopped short in his thoughts. He wondered if he should refuse to talk to the agents without having a lawyer present. These men were FBI agents. They were talking about the commission of a crime—*by Lou Powers*. "Anything you say may be used against you." Weren't they supposed to say that? They had not said it. But wasn't anything Lou said to them bound to nail down the case against him all the tighter?

The agents were watching Lou, waiting.

Lou looked to Foster for help.

Foster seemed to read his mind. His frown stayed in place, but his voice was soft, almost gentle. "Lou," he said, "I don't think you are in any trouble, if you cooperate to the fullest, and I'm sure you will."

Lou held Foster's gaze for a moment. He looked at the two FBI agents. The two young men who had greeted him with friendly smiles only a couple of minutes ago were not smiling now. Their mouths were straight lines. Their faces were blank masks. And their eyes—were his fears running away with him?—their eyes were as hard, icy as those of the best blockers trying to cut down Lou Powers on a football field.

They did not speak.

"Is that true?" Lou asked finally.

"Will you?" The question came from the agent who had told Lou he was guilty of being an accessory to a conspiracy.

"What?"

"Will you cooperate?"

The FBI was neither confirming nor rejecting Foster's opinion that Lou would not be charged if he agreed to cooperate. Lou's mind raced. The FBI agents did not have to bargain with him. They did not have to make promises. They had him cold. He had no options. He had to cooperate.

Lou glanced at Foster. Perhaps the agents had delivered the promise to Foster. How else could Foster have said what he did? "I don't think you are in any trouble, if. . . ." That had to be it.

Lou took a deep breath. Then he looked back at the agent. "Yes," he said. "I will cooperate."

"Good," the agent said. His expression did not change. "Your cooperation quite possibly—quite probably, in fact—will involve testifying in court. Do you understand?"

"I understand," Lou said.

"Good," the agent said. He leaned back in his chair. "Now begin at the beginning, please, and don't leave anything out."

The other agent reached down to a briefcase leaning against the side of the chair leg. He extracted a legal-sized pad of yellow paper and pulled a pen from his shirt pocket.

Lou told the story. He spoke slowly and chose his words carefully. He tried to use precisely the same words he had used in the first telling to Buck Foster and Scotty Hanks the evening before.

The agent taking notes interrupted occasionally, asking Lou to pinpoint times, dates, and places.

"That's it," Lou said finally.

The agent with the pad and pen kept them ready.

The other agent leaned back in a relaxed position. He nodded slightly, as if acknowledging approval of Lou's telling of the story. "You suspected Jackie because of a pass interception," he said. "Did you suspect—do you suspect—anyone else on the team?"

"No," Lou said.

The agent smiled slightly. "You answered that question pretty quickly, if you'll permit me to say so. Take a minute. Think about it."

The pictures danced through Lou's mind. Spider Willard dropped a pass. Donny Campbell fumbled. Bull Hoffman killed a drive by running on the wrong side of Jackie for a hand-off. Henry Alderman erred on the Lewiston touchdown.

"No," Lou repeated. "Nobody."

The agent nodded, as if he had received the answer he was expecting. "I played college football myself," he said. "Not the brand of football you play at Meridian, but college football, nevertheless." He smiled slightly. "I am sure that you are going to understand what I am about to say. On a football team the players become close to one another. Not always friendly, perhaps, in every case. But close, really close, in the course of several seasons of play. You come to know your teammates better than you ever knew anyone before, maybe better than you ever will know other men the rest of your life. You know their moods, their sense of humor, their aggravations, their irritations." He paused. "Do you agree with me?"

Lou nodded. "Yes," he said. He saw where the agent was leading him. He waited.

"When people, whether they are college football players or anyone else, change their way of life from right to wrong—such as taking a bribe for the first time—they undergo something of a personality change. They find themselves under stress, a new stress. It shows. Sometimes in very small ways—the way they smile, the way they joke, the way they talk. But it shows." He paused. Then, in the manner of offering an aside, he said, "When you were telling of your suspicion of Jackie, just a few minutes ago, you mentioned the expression on his face when questioned about the pass interception. He wasn't the usual cocky Jackie Manteno. You noticed a slight—very slight maybe, but very real—change in Jackie."

The agent seemed to be waiting for an answer from Lou. "Yes," Lou said finally.

The agent leaned forward, watching Lou. "Have you noticed any of that sort of change in any of your other teammates?"

Lou frowned.

"Take some time to think," the agent said.

Lou looked at the agents. Clearly, they were convinced that other players on the Browns were involved. First Jackie Manteno, then Lou Powers, now who? Tell us, Lou Powers, who else?

Lou glanced at Foster. The coach did not move. "No," Lou said. "I don't know of anything—nothing like that."

"You suspected Jackie."

"Yes, but that was a combination of things."

"What about others?"

Lou felt anger welling up in him. The agent was demanding that he point an accusing finger at a teammate

146

—at someone, anyone. Lou glanced at Foster. Still the coach said nothing, showed nothing in his expression. Lou understood Foster wanting to flush out even the smallest hint of suspicion. The coach wanted everything in the open. He wanted to clean the problem away. There was no other way to get on with the business of playing out the football schedule. But Lou resented Foster's tacit assent to the agent's relentless insistence on an accusation.

"I've told you that I don't know anything more to tell you." Lou's anger was evident in his voice. "I don't know of anyone else shaving points. I don't know of anyone else making bad plays on purpose. I don't know of anyone flashing a lot of money. And I don't know of anyone starting to act funny. It's the truth, whether you like it or not. How many times do I have to tell you?"

Nobody said anything. The silence seemed to Lou to last for minutes. He wondered, How many other Browns will be put through this kind of a grilling? How many of them will come up with a name for the agents?

Foster spoke. "Calm down, Lou. This is necessary, I'm afraid."

The agent said, "If you think of anything later, you will let us know." He was not making a request. He was issuing an order.

"Sure," Lou said.

"You will need to tell your story one more time—to a stenographer—and then sign the notarized copy."

"We will have an attorney present for that," Foster said to Lou.

147

"I think you should," the agent said.

"Sure," Lou said. "Is that all? May I go now?"

Upstairs, in the lobby of the field house, Lou encountered Spider Willard coming in the front door.

"What's going on?" Spider asked. "I got this message to come to the coach's office—like right now. I had to cut a class. What's going on?"

"Oh, God!" Lou said.

The vision of a parade of Browns appearing before the questioning, probing, demanding FBI agents—who's been acting guilty?—frightened Lou.

"Huh?" Spider asked.

"There are a couple of FBI agents in Foster's office," Lou said. "They want to know if you've been fixing the point spread or if you think anyone else has. Lovely."

Lou walked out the field-house door. He ignored the drizzling rain.

21

Lou Powers stood with the other players in the flickering light of the bonfire at the Friday night pep rally on the campus. The weather had turned chilly. All the players were wearing jackets, their collars turned up. The heat from the bonfire, carried by a light breeze, felt good to Lou.

Around the bonfire, students were standing and sitting on the layers of stone steps rising in a half circle. The Greek theater had always been the site of the Friday night bonfire rally before all home games at Meridian. The tradition reached back to the days when the outdoor theater accommodated most of the student body of the university. Now the crowd, a mix of students, faculty, and a few townspeople, extended beyond the rows of stone steps and out onto the sloping hill beyond.

Buck Foster, standing in front of the players, was speaking into a microphone. He was saying something about the importance of tomorrow's game. He was describing the Athens Tigers as a tough team, once beaten but capable of knocking off anyone on a given day.

The coach did not mention Jackie Manteno. He introduced Brad Chapman as if Brad had been the starting quarterback in the Browns' three previous games. He spoke as if there never had been a Jackie Manteno at Meridian University.

Foster did not make mention of Lou Powers' being involved in the gambling scandal. He introduced Lou, as always, with the simple description of middle linebacker and defensive captain and said nothing more.

The coach did not mention the gambling scandal at all. Nor did he mention the week's practice of the Browns. It was a subject that Foster always touched on in his pep-rally speeches. Routinely he announced that the team had worked hard and that they were ready to give their best. Always, when he said it, it was true. But this time he said nothing about the practice week. He could not say that the practice week had gone well for the Browns.

Across the way, Lou saw Paige in the crowd. She was standing with a group of girls from her dormitory. Lou tried to smile when their eyes met. It was a wan effort. Lou was finding it increasingly difficult to smile as the week dragged to an end.

For the Browns, bad had changed to worse, worse had changed to ugly. The FBI's quizzing of the players

150

had continued Tuesday, Wednesday, Thursday, even to-day. In the end, more than a dozen of the Browns, one by one, had come under the scrutiny of the two agents, the short, stocky one asking the questions, and the taller one with the yellow pad and the pen taking notes.

Lou was sure that each of the players was thinking as he went into the interview: Why me? Am I a suspect? Who pointed a finger at me? Did Lou Powers do it?

As each player returned from the interview, the questions in the minds of all the other players on the team seemed to Lou to be written clearly on their faces: What did he say in there? Was he implicated in the fix? Did he say anything to implicate anyone else? Me?

And: After the questioning, was he still on the team?

Not a one of the players, returning to the team, told what he had been asked or what he had said to the agents. And nobody asked anyone for an accounting.

For sure, they all had been asked the question: Do you have reason to suspect anyone on the team? Lou had answered no, but nobody knew it. The others had answered—what? Nobody knew.

Each day the sports pages of the newspapers and the sportscasts of the television stations trumpeted the word. The questioning was continuing at Meridian. Quarterback Jackie Manteno was gone, sure to face charges. Linebacker Lou Powers was involved. Now others were being questioned. The conclusion, although always left unstated, was clear: Others of the Meridian Browns might be involved.

The one person able to clear Lou Powers and all the

151

others remained silent. The sad-eyed little man named Charles Dryden said nothing more after naming Jackie Manteno. Undoubtedly, he had his reasons. He had made a deal of sorts, everyone said, by naming Jackie. He might name others later. But for now—silence.

The man's refusal to speak further seemed, in Lou's mind, to shout the announcement that more players on the Meridian team were involved.

The Meridian University officials repeatedly issued statements: There was no evidence indicating that other players were involved. But the statements were interpreted as expressions of hope more than strong, sound conviction.

With each passing day, the Browns functioned less like a team on the practice field. They became, with each practice session, more a collection of separate parts than the single entity that is required for football greatness. Overconfidence the previous week had almost spelled disaster for the Browns against the Lewiston Panthers. Now, on the eve of the Athens Tigers game, dissension and mistrust were brewing a more deadly mixture. In four days, the Browns had become a defiant, suspicious, defensive crew of football players, Lou Powers included.

Spider Willard, dressing for practice on Tuesday, following his unexpected interview with the FBI agents, stuck his face in Lou's and asked, "Did you give them my name? Did you tell them that they ought to talk to me?"

Lou, startled, said, "No, I—"

But Spider had turned away.

Lou, glowering at Spider's back, recalled the picture of the ace pass catcher juggling and then dropping a crucial pass against Lewiston. Perhaps Spider Willard had reason to be concerned.

In the defensive huddle on the practice field, Lou felt the eyes of his teammates—Marion Petoskey, Henry Alderman, Earl McGaha, and Mike Rushman, all of them —probing him in a different way.

They were wondering about Lou. Lou could see the doubt in their eyes. They were wondering how deeply he had been involved. They knew he had taken the money. They knew he had failed to report the incident. They knew he said he had given the money back to the gambler. They knew he said he had rejected the deal. But. . . .

They wondered, too, what Lou had said in the interview with the FBI agents. Had he implicated anyone? Lou had been the first interviewed. The others followed.

Across the line of scrimmage, Lou saw the same questioning looks among the members of the offense. Donny Campbell wondered about Bull Hoffman. Bull Hoffman wondered about Dave Emerson. Dave Emerson wondered about. . . .

Even Brad Chapman, the only starter able to claim total innocence, was not immune. Although he had not been questioned and could not possibly be involved, his face took on the same speculative look as he eyed his teammates. Brad went through the motions of directing

153

the Browns' attack in practice. But he was wondering, for sure, about all of them—Donny and Bull and Dave on the offense, Lou and Henry and Marion on the defense. The questions showed in Brad's eyes.

Blocking, always the first victim of plummeting team morale, dissolved into a mechanical act. Lou, moving in from linebacker to make the tackles, sensed the change. Gone from the blockers was the slashing ferocity, the determined effort, the bone-jarring collision that laid tacklers low and sprang runners loose. In their place were listless shoves, half-hearted bumps, and complete misses.

Then the Browns' tackling became indifferent. Ineffectual arm tackles replaced the crunching thrust of the shoulder. Ballcarriers, when they tried, faked the distracted tacklers off their feet. Tacklers, easily blocked out, did not charge back into the play. Second effort, which marks a great defense, disappeared.

Lou tried to shake himself—and his teammates, too—out of the deepening lethargy. "C'mon, Alderman, get the lead out," Lou called out, after his linebacking partner allowed a pass to get by him for a completion without more than waving a hand at the ball.

Alderman turned on Lou with a scowl on his face. "You play your position, I'll play mine," he snapped.

Buck Foster, from his raised platform, and all of the assistant coaches moving around the field barked their criticisms at the players, berating their failures and demanding a greater effort. But the sullen players responded with a shrug and nothing more.

154

As the week ended, Lou was sure that Buck Foster would call a team meeting. The air needed clearing. There were words that needed saying. Foster was the one to speak.

But Buck Foster and his assistant coaches persisted in directing the practice sessions as if nothing but a football game were occupying the minds of the Meridian Browns. Nobody, players or coaches, mentioned the corrosive underlayer of suspicion eating away at the Browns.

Puzzled, Lou grimly settled into the task of keeping his thoughts on the upcoming battle with the Athens Tigers. He drove himself harder than ever in scrimmage. He took comfort in a jolting collision. For a moment, he was a football player again, and there was no gambling scandal. The moments were rare and short-lived.

Lou, and surely the others too, knew that disaster awaited them on the field against the Athens Tigers unless the Browns found a miracle cure for mistrust and suspicion and found it quickly. Time was running out.

The dream of an undefeated season and a national championship was evaporating in the increasing heat of mistrust. A legend was blowing away on the winds of dissension based on suspicion.

And nobody was doing anything about it.

On Saturday morning, Lou rose early, dressed, and, without waiting to eat breakfast, left the Sigma Chi house. He walked the eight blocks to Buck Foster's home. He knocked on the front door, and when Foster's wife opened it, he went in.

Foster, not yet dressed for the game, was wearing jeans, a sweatshirt, a pair of worn sneakers without socks, and carrying a cup of coffee. "What is it, Lou?" Foster asked, frowning.

22

The Browns were seated around the dressing room on the benches in front of their lockers. Buck Foster was standing in the center of the dressing-room floor. The time to take the field was only minutes away. The Meridian University band could be heard in the background.

Lou knew the scene outside, although he never had seen it. Above the dressing room, all around the stadium, the last of the brown-clad fans were finding their way to their seats. Many were carrying the brown pennants that had waved more than fifty years of Meridian teams to victory. The weather was chilly but bright. Most of the fans were wearing their coats. Because of the brightness, many wore long-billed cardboard visors, brown with a golden *M* emblazoned on them. Along the sideline, a row

157

of almost twenty cheerleaders, one of them with a bull-horn, waited to lead the roar that would greet the Browns racing onto the field for the start of the game.

The battle of Meridian versus Athens was about to begin.

With a victory, the Browns would surely ride atop the national polls for another week. They would have taken one more large step toward the national championship. With a loss, they would stumble, certainly slipping from first place in the polls, perhaps never to regain the top spot. The national championship would be lost.

Foster turned slowly in the center of the dressing-room floor, frowning at the players seated around him.

The strain of the week showed in the players' faces. They wore flat, expressionless stares. The air hung heavy in the silence. There was no sparkle, no intensity, no electricity among them. Clearly, they were no better for the game today than they had been on the practice field during the week. They were going to play the game the way they had practiced—sloppily, listlessly, distractedly, troubled.

Foster cleared his throat. "We have a few minutes," he said.

Lou took a deep breath. He leaned forward on the bench, a giant of a young man, made all the larger by the huge pads strapped to his shoulders beneath the brown jersey. He sat with his elbows on his knees, hands clasped in front of him. He stared at the dressing-room floor for a second. Then he looked up, fixing his gaze on the coach.

Lou knew what was coming. He waited.

"Lou Powers came to my home this morning and suggested that he bench himself for the good of the team," Foster said. He spoke in a flat, matter-of-fact monotone. His frown never wavered. "Lou said that we are a team torn by suspicion and fear. That is true. He said that he is the center of the trouble, the focal point of the suspicions, the reason for the fears. That may be partly true too. He said that by removing himself from the team, he would be removing the stigma—the fear, the suspicion—until the investigation cleared him and everyone else. I told Powers that this was not true. I told him that the solution was not that simple. I told him that benching himself would not help the team. To the contrary, it would hurt the team."

Lou felt the glances of the players around him in the dressing room. He kept his eyes on the coach.

"Then Lou had an idea," Foster said. "And I bought it."

Foster nodded to Lou. "Lou," he said.

Foster backed up a couple of spaces and sat down on a bench, leaving the floor to Lou.

Lou kept his seat, leaning forward, elbows on his knees. He took a deep breath and glanced around the room quickly. The faces of the players ringing him were not friendly. Bull Hoffman's face was a blank. He was staring, unblinking, at Lou. Spider Willard's face seemed covered by some invisible mask, in place to deflect whatever Lou Powers was about to say. The other faces showed more: worry, suspicion, puzzlement, even antag-

159

onism. Even Donny Campbell, who should have known better, was frowning. Donny, of all of them, should have been ready to trust Lou. Even Brad Chapman, about to step back into the role of starting quarterback, looked nervous and wary.

Outside, the band had quit playing. The time for taking the field was only a few minutes away.

One of the players shuffled his feet, and the hard rubber cleats scraped the concrete floor loudly in the silence of the room.

"We're a mess," Lou said finally. He spoke softly, barely above a whisper. "A real mess, and we all know it, all of us. And we all know why. We know what's made us a mess. I know, and so do you."

Lou shifted uncomfortably and straightened himself a bit on the bench. He consciously decided to raise his voice to a conversational level.

"Sure, I suspected some of you of buying the gambler's deal," he said. "When the gambler approached me, I wondered—who else? Then I saw Jackie throw some interceptions. I saw Spider drop some passes. I saw Henry move the wrong way and allow a touchdown. I saw Bull bust a play that killed a scoring drive. I saw Donny fumble. Hell, yes, I suspected some of you."

They don't like what they're hearing. This isn't working. It's only making things worse.

Lou glanced at Foster. The coach's face, wearing the usual frown, showed nothing. Then Lou thought he detected a slight nod. He plunged ahead.

"And when everything blew up and Jackie got caught

and all that, you began suspecting people too, the same as I had done. You began wondering the same things that I had wondered: who else? You did. You know you did. Everybody was wondering about everybody else."

The faces in front of Lou were unchanged.

Are they even listening?

"We all wondered too, am *I* under suspicion? Does somebody think that *I* am on the take? Are people wondering about *me*? Then you found out about me, Lou Powers." Lou shrugged slightly. He spoke as if putting the words in parentheses. "The whole world found out about me," he said softly.

"I was a fool not to come out with it from the very start. Maybe I could have saved us this mess we are in today. But I didn't, and things got worse when everyone learned I had been approached by the gambler. Was I as innocent as I claimed? Maybe so, maybe not. Were even more players involved? Maybe so. For sure, there was more suspicion. Then I was questioned by the FBI agents. Had I pointed a finger at anyone, to save my own skin? Then others of us were questioned by the FBI agents. Was it because I had pointed a finger? Were the others, when they were being questioned, pointing at anyone? Were they deeply involved themselves? The questions were killing us."

Lou paused and took a breath. The room remained deathly quiet.

Well, here goes.

"So I asked Coach Foster if he would call the U.S. district attorney in Chicago and ask the district attorney

161

two questions: First, is there, right now, today, any other member of this team under suspicion? And, second, was there any player on this team who implicated any other player, either in the interviews with the agents or in any other way?"

They're listening now!

"Coach Foster called the district attorney this morning. He reached him at home. He explained that this football team is in trouble—deep trouble—because of the fears and suspicions. He explained that we are in real danger of seeing our whole season—maybe our careers, years of hard work—go down the tube. And maybe for no reason at all. Maybe the fears and suspicions are baseless. Could the district attorney answer the questions?"

Lou's voice rose an octave. He found himself speaking more rapidly, the words pouring out.

"Coach Foster asked the questions, and the district attorney did answer them. Then Coach Foster asked the district attorney to repeat the answers to me on the telephone. He told me: first, no, there was no evidence at the moment to indicate any other Meridian Browns were involved with the gamblers in any way. And, second, no, there was not a single member of the team who expressed a hint of suspicion about a teammate either in the formal interviews or in other reports the agents got."

Do they believe me? Lou looked around the room. Bull Hoffman's face remained blank, impassive. Spider Willard's invisible mask was still in place, but Spider was glancing around at the other players now. He was trying

162

to read their reaction while he decided his own. Donny Campbell's frown seemed to be easing away, ever so slightly. Henry Alderman stared at Lou, clearly trying to make up his mind. Buck Foster remained seated on the bench, frowning, unmoving.

Here's the last shot, the final chance.

"Spider! You thought I had turned the FBI agents onto you." Lou lifted an arm and pointed a finger at Spider. Spider's right eyebrow shot up. "You told me so. You accused me of it in the dressing room. But I didn't do it." Lou paused and took a breath. "And you didn't point at anyone either. Nobody in this room has accused anyone, and nobody in this room deserves accusing."

Lou waited. Nobody spoke.

"Don't you see?" he said finally. "We are clear of suspicion, and we are free of suspecting each other. Don't you see?"

That's it. That's all. There's nothing more.

Lou looked at the faces around him. The expressions did not change. The faces were rigid, frowning.

It didn't work.

Then there was a voice from the side of the room. "I. . . ." It was Donny Campbell.

Donny was looking at Lou. Their eyes met. Then Donny turned to Foster. He spoke to the coach. "We didn't know, and that was the bad part. We just didn't know. It was scary."

"None of us knew," Foster said curtly. "I sat in on the FBI interviews with all of you. But I did not know what they were learning elsewhere. So none of us knew—before—but we all know now."

Spider Willard got to his feet, as if to make a statement. He glanced at Lou. Spider's face was serious, still with a trace of a frown. But the invisible mask seemed gone.

A rap at the door stopped Spider, and a voice called out from the corridor, "Coach Foster, kickoff time."

Foster got to his feet and gestured Spider into silence. "We haven't got time for a round of speeches," he said. "I don't like speeches anyway. One ought to be enough. It's been a long and hard week for us. But it's all over now. Let's just say that everyone in this room has apologized to everyone else, and go out and play a football game."

Foster walked toward the dressing-room door.

Lou got to his feet, waiting for the signal for him, as defensive captain of the Browns, to lead the team onto the field.

Foster fixed his frown on Lou, seeming to be waiting for something.

"Well," Lou said, and stopped.

Foster nodded slightly.

"Let's remember," Lou said, "we *are* the Meridian Browns."

Foster opened the dressing-room door, and Lou jogged through. The other players streamed out behind him.

The fans jamming the stadium rose to their feet with a roar when the Browns came out of the ramp and onto the field. At the far corner of the field, the Meridian band

164

broke into the Browns' fight song as the players ran past the line of whooping cheerleaders toward their bench. Along the sideline, a television camera crew wheeled slowly along the cinder track, keeping pace with the advancing players, the eye of the camera on the linebacker leading the way.

Not one of the fans in the stadium, not one of the cheerleaders shouting the players on, not a person in the television audience across the country knew that a hallowed Meridian football tradition had just been broken. For the first time in more years than anyone could remember, the Meridian Browns' coach had not been the one who sent the players onto the field with the words: "Remember, you *are* the Meridian Browns."

This time Lou Powers had said them.

23

Johnny Douglass boomed the game's opening kickoff through the end zone, and the Athens Tigers started their offense on the twenty-yard line, without benefit of a runback.

"A good beginning," Lou said to himself, as he led his defense onto the field to meet the Tigers' first thrust.

"Get 'em," Brad Chapman sang out from the sideline, as Lou jogged away.

Lou waved a hand in acknowledgment.

Coming from Brad, the shouted words of encouragement were more than a cheer, Lou knew. The events of the past week left the Browns needing a sturdy defense more than ever. Brad Chapman had stepped into the role of starting quarterback only five days ago. Despite his quarterbacking abilities, Brad was a strange hand at the controls of the Meridian attack. The timing was going to be different. The hand-offs were going to have an unfamiliar quality. The passes were going to feel differently to the receivers. For the Browns' offense, there was going to be a change of pace. It was unavoidable, and it was bound to hurt. To make up the difference, the Browns needed the advantage, delivered by a good defense, of taking over the ball in good field position every time. Only a great game by the defense could do the job.

Lou glanced at his crew in the defense huddle. He wondered if they doubted their burden—facing a tough team, coming off a bad practice week, working with a new quarterback. To score, the Browns needed an outstanding performance from the defense.

Henry Alderman, Mike Rushman, Earl McGaha, Marion Petoskey—all of them—looked at Lou with serious faces, waiting for him to call the defensive signal.

Lou said simply, "Fullback up the middle, you know."

The Tigers' first play from scrimmage might just as well have been broadcast on the stadium loudspeaker. The play would be a straight hand-off to the fullback charging into the middle of the line. The conservative Athens Tigers made a fetish of opening every game with a simple plunge into the middle of the line. The Tigers liked the basics of football. They believed in muscle against muscle in the middle of the line. They always wanted, and got, the quickest possible test of strength.

The Athens quarterback lined up behind the center, stared blankly at the Meridian defense for a moment, then barked his signals and took the snap from center.

The instant the quarterback turned to his right, with the ball extended, Lou leaped toward the charging form of Norm Jordan, struggling to beat off a blocker. The play was going into Norm's side of the line.

The fullback, a square-built, low-slung power driver, took the hand-off from the quarterback and steamrollered into the line with his heavy legs pumping hard. Norm lunged over a blocker and got hold of one of the fullback's driving legs.

At that moment, Lou crashed head on into the fullback, hitting him just above the waist. For what seemed like minutes, the two powerful bodies strained against each other in their position, neither of them yielding.

Then with a grunt the fullback surrendered. Lou drove him back and over and fell on top of him. Norm, still clutching the fullback's leg, tumbled backward with them.

In the grandstands, the Meridian fans got to their feet with a cheer. The beauty of superb defense provided the greatest thrills the game had to offer for Meridian fans, and they cheered the perfect defensive play.

The referee placed the ball just beyond the twenty-yard line, a gain of less than a yard for the hard-driving fullback. The Athens Tigers had run their game-opening test. And the Meridian Browns, in the form of line-backer Lou Powers, had won it.

Lou knew there were many other stern tests to come. He and his defense were in for a long afternoon. The

Tigers' bruising style of play relied on strong blocking and powerful running. The Tigers seldom passed. They hardly ever indulged themselves in anything even fairly resembling trickery. They preferred instead to slam into the line or come crashing around the ends with a fleet of blockers leading the way. The Tigers' way of playing football guaranteed the Browns' defense a physical battering.

The opening play of the game did, indeed, set the tone for the Tigers' strategy. The game quickly took on the qualities of a textbook defensive classic. The Browns' mighty defense staved off the line plunges and end sweeps of the Athens Tigers. And the Tigers' defense, facing a Browns' attack that was less than it might have been, contained the running of Bull Hoffman and Donny Campbell and clamped a lid on Brad Chapman's passing.

By half time the scoreboard showed: 0-0.

The two teams had pounded at each other between the thirty-yard lines. There were no major errors by either team. There was no luck for either team. There was only the collision of strong bodies, the test of skill against skill, a battle of determination.

For both teams, the missing ingredient was the breakthrough play—a fumble recovery deep in the opponent's territory, a pass interception and a long runback, a runner suddenly bursting through the line and breaking into the clear.

Buck Foster told the Browns as much in the dressing room before they returned to the field for the second

169

half. "There is a good chance this game is going to be won by one play," he said. "Don't give it to them. Make them give it to you."

The ball was on the Athens forty-six-yard line, third down and one yard to go for the Tigers for a first down. The third quarter was five minutes old.

Lou blinked at the scoreboard at the top of the stadium beyond the end zone: still, 0-0. For Lou, the next play of the Athens Tigers was easy to forecast: Somebody, perhaps even the quarterback himself, was going to plunge into the middle of the line, trying to gain the one yard needed for a first down to keep the drive alive.

With the snap of the ball, Lou hurled himself into the melee at the center of the line. His shoulder crashed into a red helmet. He grabbed. He shoved and twisted, turning the body in his grasp to the side, and he rode the body to the ground. Lou knew before he got up that the quarterback, trying a keeper, had fallen short of the one precious yard that he needed.

The referee decided that the quarterback had lost half a yard.

It was fourth down, and the Tigers' punting team came onto the field.

Behind Lou, Donny Campbell awaited the punt at the Browns' ten-yard line. Donny was dancing a nervous jig. The memory of another kick—and a fumble—flashed through Lou's mind. He hoped that Donny was not remembering.

At the snap, Lou began fading backward, setting

170

himself to block an Athens tackler and help clear a path for Donny's runback.

The punter sent a high spiral soaring toward the goal. Donny took a step forward, then another, and gathered in the ball on the eleven-yard line.

With the high, floating punt eating up seconds, the Athens tacklers were thundering in on Donny by the time he got his hands on the ball. Another kick returner might have signaled for a fair catch, saving himself the risk of a bone-rattling tackle. But Donny was not about to call for a fair catch and leave the Browns with their backs to the wall in a scoreless game. He ducked the first tackler who came crashing in.

Racing toward the sideline, Donny gave up yardage to elude another pair of tacklers. He was back on the six-yard line. Penned in, he reversed his field, giving up yardage again in a desperate effort to break loose. He was back on the three-yard line. Trapped, he turned again. A block by Dave Emerson saved him from a tackler. He ran along the goal line, trying to reach the magical point where he might turn his speed upfield.

He never made it. Two tacklers burst in on him, pinned him in, and slammed him to the ground in the end zone.

Lou was leaping back to his feet after throwing a block. He looked around quickly to see where the action was heading. He saw Donny disappear under the pile of white jerseys with red trim.

The scoreboard blinked: Browns 0, Visitors 2. Donny had been caught behind the goal for a safety.

Lou ran toward Donny, leaving the field. Tears were streaming down the little flanker back's cheeks, and he was pumping his fists in frustration.

Lou draped an arm around Donny's shoulders. "Don't worry," he said. "We'll get those points back."

Brad Chapman came off the sideline and met them. Then Bull Hoffman. Then Spider Willard. Henry Alderman jogged up to them from behind.

Hands touched Donny from all sides.

By the time Donny reached the sideline, he was barely visible in the crowd of teammates escorting him from the field.

24

The scoreboard showed the start of the fourth quarter. Beneath the clock the lights still read: Browns 0, Visitors 2.

All around the stadium, there was a tense silence. Along the Browns' sideline, the only movement was the jerky pacing of Buck Foster. Scowling through his glasses at the action on the field, saying nothing, he was searching for the breakthrough play.

The players, all of them on their feet, watched the play in silence.

The two teams had spent the third quarter as they had spent the first half—probing and punting, keeping each other bottled up between the thirty-yard stripes. The Meridian defense gave the Tigers no openings. But the Browns' attack, being guided by a quarterback only one week into the role, sputtered too often. Missing were the explosiveness for a long touchdown strike and the consistency for a drive to the goal.

Lou, lining up for the next play, feared that the one big breakthrough play of the game already had occurred. The Tigers were leading by those two points they had scored by nailing Donny Campbell in the end zone for a safety. They might win the game by those two points.

It was a ridiculous score for a football game. Nobody could lose a football game, and lose the national championship probably, by a score of 2–0. But there it was, up on the scoreboard in lights. And now the fourth quarter was ticking away.

The ball was on the Tigers' own forty-one-yard line. It was third down and six yards to go for a first down.

The Tigers were going to run the ball, for sure. The Tigers always ran the ball, Lou reflected. He braced himself for another jolting collision with a blocker and then maybe with the churning legs of the Tigers' tireless fullback.

The quarterback took the snap from center and stepped back. He straightened suddenly and cocked his arm. The movement froze Lou in his position for a moment. He waited to protect his zone against a pass. The quarterback pumped his arm once in a quick pass fake. Then he brought the ball down. He turned and handed off to the fullback. Lou, with a moment lost to the pass fake, threw himself toward the fullback. The Tigers' center was rolling in on Lou with a block. Lou, struggling forward, reached over the blocker and got his hands on the fullback's shoulders. Hanging on, he slowed the fullback's powerful thrust. Max Schellenbarger, coming off a block, knifed through and slammed into the fullback. The fullback's forward charge carried him another yard before he went to the ground.

A four-yard gain. Pretty good yardage for the Tigers in this kind of game. But not good enough for a first down. The Tigers were two yards short. The Browns had stopped them again.

The Tigers' punter sent a spiral to Donny Campbell on the sixteen-yard line. Donny gathered in the ball and, behind a devastating block by Dave Emerson, raced back to the Browns' thirty-one-yard line.

Lou, walking off the field, passed the offensive unit moving in. Nobody spoke.

At the sideline, Buck Foster held Brad Chapman back a moment from the group taking the field. Another player stood with the quarterback and the coach. Foster, shorter than either of his players, standing between them, his back to the playing field, had a hand resting on a shoulder of each player as he spoke. The players were listening, motionless.

Brad then nodded and broke away and raced onto the field to take up the attack. The other player stepped back and took up a position on the sideline to watch the play. He was Johnny Douglass.

Lou knew what they had been discussing—a quick kick by Johnny, catching the Tigers by surprise and sending them reeling back deep in their own territory. The Browns practiced the quick kick every week of the season. They seldom used the play. But they were always ready with the weapon.

Brad was going to run two plays, hoping to improve the Browns' field position from their own thirty-one-yard line. If the Browns got a first down, Johnny Douglass could relax for a moment. Brad would then move the Browns into another series of downs, hoping to keep the drive going.

But if the Browns failed to get a first down, Johnny would go into the game at the fullback position. With luck, the Tigers would not notice that the new fullback was also the Browns' punter. Then, in a normal formation, the center would snap the ball through Brad's legs to Johnny, and a booming kick would soar over the heads of the surprised Athens defenders. With a good bounce and roll, and no runback, the Tigers would be left with their backs to their own goal. Then it would become the job of the Browns' defense to hold the Tigers in the hole or shove them deeper into the hole and regain possession of the ball in good position for the offense.

The quick kick is the ultimate accolade for a team's defense. When a team spends one of its ball-possession downs to quick kick, it is saying to the opponent: "Here's the ball. Go ahead and take it. Our defense is good enough to hold and throw you back." No team with a leaky defense can afford to give the ball away to an opponent. But a team with a staunch defense can make yardage and points by handing over the ball with a quick kick.

Foster was pulling the weapon out of the Browns' arsenal in an attempt to force the big breakthrough play the Browns so desperately needed.

On the first play, Brad zipped a pass to Spider in the right flat. The gangly end, twisting and spinning, fought his way to the Browns' forty-yard line—a gain of nine yards. Bull Hoffman hit the center for two yards and a first down on the Browns' forty-two-yard line.

Lou, standing at the sideline, glanced at Johnny Douglass. The kicker seemed to sigh. The first down delayed his role in the strategy.

Donny scampered around end for three yards and Dave got two yards off tackle, bringing up third down and five to go, on the Browns' forty-seven-yard line.

Buck Foster gestured four players into the game— Johnny Douglass, plus three linemen going along solely to make a crowd. Johnny's entry had a better chance of escaping notice if he was one of several taking the field.

Quickly the Browns lined up.

Brad barked the signals—a short count to hold to the minimum the number of seconds the Tigers would have to spot Johnny Douglass and recognize what was coming. But Brad's count was not quick enough.

Suddenly, from the Tigers' side of the line, a shout rang out "Quick kick!"

The left-side linebacker had noted and identified the new player in the Browns' backfield. He leaped forward to a position up close to the line to join the charge to block the kick. Behind them, defensive halfbacks were backpedaling furiously.

Steve Sherman sent the snap through Brad's legs to Johnny. The snap, a low bullet, was perfect. Brad joined Steve's forward push, blocking the onrushing Athens linemen in the center of the line.

Johnny took the snap just above knee level. He took one short step. He booted the ball. The flying form of a Tiger lineman breaking through was a blur in front of Johnny. Arms high, the lineman tried to block the ball. He missed.

The kick got away, a low, wobbling spiral. It was going to be a short kick. But it was over the head, barely, of the scrambling Athens defensive halfback. The halfback turned in frantic pursuit of the ball.

The Browns' linemen were breaking through and rushing downfield to cover the ball or tackle a ballcarrier. The ball hit the ground on the nineteen-yard line. It took a funny bounce toward the goal—a good bounce, Lou thought—and then crazily reversed itself on the second bounce, caroming off the chest of a startled Athens player chasing it.

Having been touched by an Athens player, it was a free ball. The ball disappeared under a pile of bodies. Players on the edge of the pile jumped around nervously. All of them signaled wildly that their team, not the other, had possession of the ball, as if their determination and enthusiasm could make it so.

The referee bent into the crowd and picked his way through the tangle of arms and legs.

Lou stepped forward at the sideline, staring at the scene.

Finally the referee rose and lifted his arm in a mighty wave—Browns' ball on the Tigers' fourteen-yard line. Lou threw his fist into the air and let out a cheer. A roar from the grandstand rolled down over the field.

Even if the touchdown effort failed in three downs, Johnny Douglass could boot a field goal, giving the Browns a 3–2 lead.

Buck Foster, his back to the field, was shouting instructions into the ear of a guard, who would carry the series of plays into the huddle.

On the field, Steve Sherman, smiling and waving his arms above his head, emerged dancing from the pile of bodies on the ground. The Browns' center had fought his way out of the crowd at the line of scrimmage and raced downfield to recover the loose ball.

The players on the field mobbed Steve, slapping his shoulder pads and his helmet, while he continued to leap and pump his hands in the air. Brad finally grabbed him to set up the huddle and regroup the offense.

After a quick moment in the huddle, the Browns lined up. Brad had Bull Hoffman directly behind him in the fullback position. Donny and Dave were to his right, Donny spread wide and Dave close in. At end, Spider was split out wide.

Brad took the snap and backpedaled, handing off to Bull.

The draw play up the middle got three yards to the Tigers' eleven-yard line.

The Browns lined up again in the same formation, again giving the impression they were going to flood the right side with pass receivers.

With the snap, Brad backpedaled and again handed the ball to Bull Hoffman. But this time Brad retrieved the ball. Bull charged into the line empty-handed, faking a plunge. Brad turned to his left with the ball. Donny, crossing over, was racing for the intersection of the goal line and the sideline. Brad shoveled the ball out to Donny.

Donny took in the ball on the dead run, then cut sharply to the inside. Running against the grain of the off-balance Tigers' defense, he slipped through into the end zone, barely touched.

The Browns standing at the sideline charged onto the field and met the grinning Donny coming off the field. Lou, reaching out a hand to pat Donny's shoulder, saw the sparkling eyes and the laughing face. It seemed ages ago that Lou had seen the same face twisted in frustration at his failure, with tears streaming down his cheeks.

Johnny Douglass' kick for the extra point was good. The scoreboard blinked and settled into: Browns 7, Visitors 2.

Buck Foster waved down the cheering at the sideline. He repeated over and over as he paced, "This game is not won yet. This game is not won yet."

Lou agreed. He glanced at the clock on the scoreboard. There were seven minutes and forty-two seconds remaining in the game. The Athens Tigers had plenty of time. If they scored, they would win the game. There would not be time for the Browns to come from behind again. Watching the teams line up for the kickoff, Lou snapped his helmet strap and prepared to take the field.

The victory for the Browns was going to depend on the defense, the pride of the Meridian Browns for more than fifty years.

25

The Athens Tigers lined up for the kickoff with two players, instead of their usual one, standing on the ten-yard line to receive the ball.

Johnny Douglass' kick backed up the receivers to the four-yard line. The player on the near side received the kick. Then he and his partner crossed, reversing their fields, and the ballcarrier handed off to the other player. It was an old, old trick, but an effective one. It forced the onrushing tacklers to swerve to follow the ball, losing a step in the process.

Lou, staring at the play from his position on the sideline, saw trouble shaping up right away. As the ball-carrier, a speedster, scampered toward the sideline in a swooping arc pointing upfield, a wall of blockers materialized. They sealed off the sideline, creating a corridor for the ballcarrier dancing along the sideline.

The Athens ballcarrier raced all the way to the Tigers' forty-one-yard line—a thirty-seven-yard return—before a Browns' defender crashed through and knocked him out of bounds.

Lou jogged onto the field to take up his defensive position. The Tigers had good field position for their final, frantic push for a touchdown. Lou glanced at the scoreboard. The lights read 7–2; the clock showed just seven minutes remaining.

On the Athens sideline, the Tigers' coach was holding the quarterback by the arm, shouting into his ear above the roar of the crowd. Then the coach slapped the quarterback on the rump and sent him dashing onto the field.

Lou stared at the quarterback across the line of scrimmage and braced himself for the first thrust.

The roar from the Meridian fans was deafening. Rhythmically they chanted, "No gain! No gain! No gain at all!"

The Athens quarterback finally stepped back and waved his arms in futility at the referee. He complained that his teammates could not hear his signals in the roar of the crowd. The roar got louder, mixed with laughter.

The referee waved at both sides of the field, and the noise died away.

The quarterback stepped back into position, barked his signals, took the snap and spun to Lou's left. Lou instinctively drifted to his left, following the flow of the

183

play. The quarterback extended the ball to the work-horse fullback. The fullback slammed into the line off tackle. His legs pumping like pistons, he forced himself between tackle and end and crashed into Henry Alderman. The fullback's legs still were driving when he fell to the ground in Henry's grasp, just as Lou came rocketing into the scene. He had made a four-yard gain, to the Tigers' forty-five-yard line.

Lou had been expecting something more explosive—a reverse perhaps or at least a pass.

But now he knew: The Athens Tigers won their games, week in and week out, with a methodical, physical style of football. They tried no tricks. They took as few chances as possible. They ran hard, they blocked hard, and they counted on the combination to win for them. Usually it did. Now they were determined to win this game the same way. They might go to the air or try some razzle-dazzle if the clock started running out on them. But not now. Not with seven minutes remaining. They still had time to stick to their game plan. The Tigers could win the game with four-yard gains. They could march all the way to the goal with four-yard gains. Nothing spectacular, to be sure, but effective.

The thought troubled Lou as he settled into position. Seldom were the Athens Tigers held without a single touchdown by any team. But the Meridian Browns had to do it today to win.

The Tigers, as if validating Lou's fears, reeled off a series of gainers: an end run for six yards, a pair of short gains—two yards and five yards—by the fullback, a quick pass in the seam between Lou and Henry for five yards.

Suddenly the Tigers stood on the Browns' thirty-seven-yard line with a first down. The battering-ram style of football was moving the Tigers down the field.

The stadium was silent now, except for the small red-clad crowd of Athens fans, waving their banners and standing in the excitement of seeing their team on the move.

Lou gathered his defense around him.

"How much time left?" somebody asked.

"The clock doesn't matter," Lou snapped.

Heads that were halfway turned to look at the clock beyond the end zone turned back to Lou.

"We've got to stop them, and we've got to do it right here, right now," Lou said. "No gain. We stop 'em cold. Understand? No gain."

The heads nodded. The faces around Lou wore serious expressions.

The defense moved into position as the Tigers were breaking their huddle. The Athens quarterback knelt behind his center, spoke the signals, took the snap, and whirled. Lou waited a moment, watching. The quarterback handed off to a halfback racing toward the sideline, to Lou's left.

Henry Alderman moved forward to meet the play. Lou ran parallel to the line of scrimmage, in the linebacker's corridor, to back up Henry and Max Schellenbarger, now fighting their way through the blockers.

Lou cut in sharply through a hole left by a guard

who had pulled to help lead the blocking interference around end. Shoving aside a back trying to block the hole, Lou advanced toward the ballcarrier from the side.

Max and Henry tangled with the blockers. The ballcarrier slowed his pace, waiting to see which way the flailing bodies would go, looking for his opening. The moment's delay by the ballcarrier was all that Lou needed.

Leaning forward, legs driving, Lou crashed into the halfback with a shoulder to the ribs. He heard the familiar sound of collision—pop!—and he heard the grunt of the halfback with all the breath going out of him. The halfback collapsed on his side with Lou driving him into the ground.

Getting to his feet, Lou looked at the sideline marker and glanced at the referee. The halfback had not gained a single inch—no gain.

On the next play, second down and still ten yards to go, Lou fixed his gaze on the fullback. The Tigers needed a sure gainer. The fullback was their meal-ticket ballcarrier. The fullback was sure to be the quarterback's choice.

On a short count, the quarterback took the snap, turned, and handed to the fullback thundering over guard to Lou's right.

Lou moved the instant the fullback veered slightly. The veer tipped the side of the line the fullback was hitting. Earl McGaha, double blocked up front in the Tigers' effort to make a hole for the fullback, was in

186

trouble. But Lou got there, with Marion Petoskey right behind him, at the moment the fullback arrived. The fullback's forward motion stopped as if he had collided with a concrete wall. Lou, slightly high, hit the fullback in the chest with a shoulder and wrapped his arms around him, bracing his feet in a wide stance for the jolt of the collision. Marion threw himself at the fullback at thigh level. Together, they threw the fullback backward.

The fullback had made it to the line of scrimmage, but no farther. It was no gain. Third down and ten yards to go.

Lou fought a desire to look at the clock. It must be showing only four or five minutes remaining in the game. Still time for the Tigers to score if they were not stopped here. But no time for another chance if the Browns took the ball away from them.

"Watch for a pass," Lou said in the defensive huddle. He spoke automatically. Even the conservative Tigers would have to go to the air on third and ten with time running out.

The Tigers made no secret of their plans to pass. They lined up in a spread formation the Browns had not seen before. The flankers were out wide. The fullback was in position behind the quarterback, ready to block.

On either side of Lou, Henry and Marion stepped out a few paces to cover the threat of the flankers.

The quarterback took the snap and backpedaled without bothering to fake a running play. He looked to his right, cocking his arm. Lou held his position, waiting. Up front, the linemen were struggling to break through. The quarterback turned to his left. He fired a short bullet pass toward the sideline. Lou turned and ran in the direction of the throw. Ahead of him, he saw Marion Petoskey, a hand up, reaching for the ball. Marion got a piece of the ball, deflecting it upward. The ball, slowed in its path, seemed to float. Marion, in his lunge, fell to the ground. The Athens flanker screeched to a halt, turned, and leaped for the falling ball. He got his fingers on it, but that was all, and the ball dropped to the ground.

Incomplete pass—no gain. Fourth down and ten yards to go.

Lou glanced at the Athens bench. Would the Tigers send in a punting unit and hope for the best? Perhaps the Browns would fumble a punt. Or perhaps, with their backs to the wall, the Browns would fumble on a play from scrimmage. The Tigers could find themselves with new life in the shadow of the goal in the waning seconds of the game. Maybe, even if the Browns did not fumble, the Tigers could make good use of their time-outs, hold the Browns for three downs, and get the ball back in time to score. Teams had won in the past with such strategy.

There was no action on the Tigers' bench. They were going to go for it. After almost sixty minutes of play, the difference between victory and defeat came down to one play.

188

"A pass, for sure," Lou told the defense huddle. "This time, I'm going in."

The players nodded.

Henry and Marion would need to close ranks slightly to guard the middle left vacant by Lou.

Lou's decision was a gamble. But he was betting on a well-honed instinct. The Tigers' linemen would not be expecting a linebacker blitz. On fourth down and ten, at this stage in the game, a pass was certain. With a pass certain, the linebackers surely would be drifting back, guarding their zones. They would not be blitzing, leaving a gap in the pass defense. The Tigers' linemen, Lou was sure, would not be expecting him to come hurtling at them. With the advantage of surprise, he had hopes of success.

When the center snapped the ball to the quarterback, Lou leaped forward. He clawed his way past the center who was concentrating on stopping Earl McGaha.

Over the shoulders of the blockers in the backfield, Lou's eyes and the quarterback's eyes met for a brief instant. The quarterback saw disaster roaring in on him. Lou read the message in the quarterback's eyes.

A blocker sailed at Lou and missed him completely. A second blocker was better. He tried a stand-up block that slowed Lou's rush. Then he lowered himself and rolled into Lou's legs, trying to cut him down. Lou shoved downward with his hands, driving the blocker to the ground. Then Lou sidestepped the blocker and took off after the unprotected quarterback.

The quarterback tried to scramble away from Lou. But Lou got a hand on him. He held on. He got the other arm around him. They fell to the ground.

Lou looked up and saw the smiling face of Earl McGaha. The burly guard was extending a hand to him. Lou took it and got to his feet.

"I think that one was for no gain too," Earl said.

Lou nodded and turned to walk off the field. The offense was coming on to take possession of the ball. Lou heard the roar of the standing crowd as he walked slowly toward the bench. He heard, too, the ghosts of the great Meridian defenses of the past. They were satisfied.

Buck Foster stepped to the center of the dressing-room floor, the game ball held easily in his right hand.

Lou, at his locker, was peeling off his jersey. He turned, his shoulder pads still covering his broad shoulders, and watched the coach.

The dressing room was silent.

There had been a strange silence since the end of the game. There had been no whooping and cheering by the victorious Browns. Even the adding of another touchdown in the closing seconds did not turn on the laughter and chatter of the winning dressing room. Thanks to a thirty-two-yard burst through the line by Bull Hoffman and then a twenty-three-yard scamper by Donny Campbell for his second score, the Browns increased their margin to 14–2 and won going away. Still, there was none of the winners' cheerful exhilaration. Instead, there

190

was a sense of satisfied weariness, quiet fulfillment. They had pulled themselves together after a week of divisive suspicion and had won the game. They had played without the quarterback they were used to—a player who sold them out—and still they had won. It felt good. But it was not a time for laughter.

Foster, without a word, walked forward and handed the game ball to Lou.

Lou took the ball in both hands. He looked down at it for a moment. Then he handed the ball to his right, to Max Schellenbarger. Max handed the ball to Henry Alderman. Henry passed it to Brad Chapman. Brad gave the ball to Spider Willard. Spider to Dave Emerson, Dave to Bull Hoffman, Bull to Norm Jordan—all the way around the room.

The last player, Earl McGaha, extended the ball to Lou.

"No," Lou said.

Earl shrugged slightly and handed the ball back to Foster.

Foster stood for a moment with the ball in his hands. "I'll find a place for it," he said finally. With a slight nod, he turned and walked to the coaches' dressing room, carrying the ball.

Lou stepped out of the dressing-room door into the usual roaring throng of fans and sportswriters jammed into the corridor. He spotted Brad Chapman's father, smiling now. Lou returned the smile.

"Who won the game ball?" a reporter shouted.

Lou looked at the man. "We did," he said. "The Meridian Browns."

The reporter, his pencil ready to jot the name in his notebook, looked up, puzzled.

Then Lou saw Paige at the edge of the crowd, and he made his way toward her.